"I'm happy to see you again, Mr. Turner."

A shiver ran up his spine and he swallowed hard. "Me, too, ma'am. I mean... I'm happy to see ya."

She smiled. "I understood what you meant. Shall we go into the dining room?"

"Uh-huh," he said, never taking his eyes off of her.

"Then that means we'll have to walk there," she pointed out.

"Oh. Yeah." He took a step back. "Plumb forgot about that part."

She smiled as her shoulders shook with silent laughter. Lord help him, but he'd already managed to make a fool of himself, and they hadn't even sat down to supper yet. He offered her his arm. "May I escort ya in?"

Her smile softened, and she wrapped her arm around his. "Thank you."

Eli's heart swelled at the contact. Never had he seen such a beautiful woman. And to think she would be his, every last lovely inch. So what if she couldn't cook or sew or clean yet? At the moment, he didn't care.

Kit Morgan has written all her life. Her whimsical stories are fun, inspirational, sweet and clean, and depict a strong sense of family and community. Raised by a homicide detective, one would think she'd write suspense, but no. Kit likes fun and romantic Westerns! Kit resides in the beautiful Pacific Northwest in a little log cabin on Clear Creek, after which her fictional town that appears in many of her books is named.

DEAR MR. TURNER

KIT MORGAN

Recycling programs
for this product may
not exist in your area.

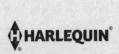

ISBN-13: 978-1-335-93736-0

Dear Mr. Turner

First published in 2016 by Kit Morgan. This edition published in 2020.
Copyright © 2016 by Kit Morgan

For questions and comments about the quality of this book,
please contact us at CustomerService@Harlequin.com.

Harlequin Enterprises ULC
22 Adelaide St. West, 40th Floor
Toronto, Ontario M5H 4E3, Canada
www.Harlequin.com

Printed in U.S.A.

DEAR MR. TURNER

Prologue

Denver, Colorado, 1901

"Fantine!" a voice called from another room. The accent was odd—Deep South overlaid with French. "When you're done dusting, do prepare a pot of tea!"

Fantine Le Blanc, assistant to the eccentric matchmaker Adelia Pettigrew, sighed. "*Oui, Madame!*" she called back in her native French accent.

Fantine had been in Mrs. Pettigrew's employ not three weeks and had already become the brunt of many a joke around town. She knew her mistress could be, shall we say, a little odd, but there was no need for name-calling. Unfortunately, every time she went to the nearby mercantile or butcher shop or when she picked up the laundry, she heard whispers behind her back as she passed. At least they weren't telling them to her face.

Okay, a few had…but she really didn't know what the problem was. Besides, if the folks in town doing the name-calling would take the time to get to know Mrs.

Pettigrew better, they'd see she wasn't so bad. Fantine didn't think she was. The woman was just…different.

So she smoked cigars—what of it? So she dressed somewhat…flamboyantly? When one had as much money as Mrs. Pettigrew, one could dress any way one pleased, Fantine supposed. And having tea with her dog, *Monsieur* Pickles, along with a few neighborhood pooches shouldn't be counted as unconventional. Mrs. Pettigrew saw it as a charity, feeding the poor things seven days per week at precisely four in the afternoon. She couldn't let the pups starve. Not that they were— most belonged to some neighbor or another.

But no one else saw things the way Fantine had come to during her time at the Pettigrew mansion on the hill. Granted, the first week was a bit rough…

"Fantine!"

Fantine jumped and almost fell off the chair she'd been standing on. "*Oui, Madame.*"

"Tea, I said! Tea! The doggies are waiting!" Mrs. Pettigrew entered her home office.

"But I thought I was to finish the dusting first?"

"Oh. I did tell you that, didn't I?"

Fantine turned on her perch and stared at her employer, wide-eyed. Mrs. Pettigrew had changed out of her day dress and now wore a gown of the brightest pink she'd ever seen. "Are you going to a party?"

"Of course not, only tea. Now if you would be so kind as to prepare it?"

"Right away, *Madame.*" She turned back to the framed letters she'd been dusting on the wall, and one in particular caught her eye. "*Madame* Pettigrew?"

"Yes, *ma cherie*?"

"Do you remember the story you told me of *Mon-*

sieur Weaver and his bride Ebba? It was the first day I was here."

"Yes, what about them?"

Fantine tucked the feather duster under one arm then carefully removed the framed letter from the wall. "You were going to tell me the story of this one, but never did."

"Oh?" Mrs. Pettigrew took a few steps closer. "Which one are you referring to?"

Fantine smiled as she climbed off the chair. "This one."

Mrs. Pettigrew took the letter from her and began to read. "Ohhhh yes, Mr. Turner! I'd quite forgotten. I am so sorry, *ma belle*."

"When it is convenient for you, *Madame* Pettigrew, I would very much like to hear it."

"Then fix our pot of tea and join us. I shall then regale you and our guests with the whole story!"

Fantine tentatively smiled as she pictured sitting at the low table where Mrs. Pettigrew served the dogs tea. It was obviously made for children, and Fantine often wondered if Mrs. Pettigrew had purchased it for the child she never had, her husband having died before they were blessed with any. "I will hurry to prepare the pot, *Madame*."

Mrs. Pettigrew smiled. "See that you do."

Fantine curtsied and hurried to comply.

When the tea was done, she put everything she needed on a tray, brought it into the sitting room—one of several—and set it on the low table. Several dogs were running around, barking and playing. Mrs. Pettigrew gave a loud whistle, and Fantine watched in fascination as the hounds gathered around the table, tails wagging. They knew what was coming.

"Don't dawdle, Fantine," Mrs. Pettigrew scolded. "Serve the tea!"

Fantine poured Mrs. Pettigrew a cup, then handed her the pot. The woman deftly placed saucers in front of each dog and poured a small amount of tea into them. Fantine tried not to laugh as the animals sniffed at the tea and tried to lap it up, but it was still too hot. She'd seen this many times by now and each time it was just as hysterical. Several of the dogs didn't bother at this point, knowing that if they waited, the tea would be cooler. The rest were more interested in the treat that would come next. Some, being dogs, didn't care for tea at all.

Mrs. Pettigrew motioned to Fantine to serve the cookies. She went around the table and placed one next to each dog's saucer. Mrs. Pettigrew had her put them in the tea cups a few times, but too much china got broken when the dogs pushed them off the table trying to get to their treat. This new method worked much better.

Fantine finished her task, poured herself a cup and sat on a cushion on the floor as Mrs. Pettigrew was doing. The dogs went silent except for their tails thumping on the carpet as they looked intently at Mrs. Pettigrew. She smiled, gave a low whistle and they attacked their treats with gusto.

"Now, *ma petit*, you wish to hear the story of *Monsieur* Turner?"

Fantine fought the urge to cringe as dogs licked the table to get every last crumb. "Yes, *Madame*, I would."

"Well then, we must begin at the beginning!"

Fantine pulled her gaze from the dogs and looked at her. "Of course, *Madame*."

"If you recall, *Monsieur* Turner lived in a town called Clear Creek in Oregon. Sheriff Hughes from my last story was also from there."

"Yes, I remember. He married Mary Weaver, and the young deputy Tom was to replace him as sheriff in Clear Creek."

"Right you are, my dear. And so he did."

"Is this story about Tom Turner? I thought he was already married."

"Indeed he is. No, this is about his younger brother. Eli."

"Oh," Fantine said with a nod. "And who was his bride?"

Mrs. Pettigrew smiled as two of the dogs started lapping up tea. "Pleasant Comfort."

Fantine's entire face screwed up. "Pleasant…who?"

"Comfort. That was her name."

Fantine's mouth fell open. "Who names a child such a thing?"

"A clever woman, that's who!"

Fantine sighed. Naturally Mrs. Pettigrew would think it clever.

"But it gets better. Some of Pleasant's brothers—she had six brothers, you know—also had clever names. The oldest was Major Quincy Comfort—"

Fantine's eyes grew wide. "Are you serious?"

"*Oui*. That is his name to this day."

Fantine fought the urge to roll her eyes. If she'd been given such a name, she never would have kept it? "He never changed it to something else?"

"Of course not. Why would he?" Mrs. Pettigrew asked

in shock. "Her other brothers' names were not so special," she continued with a dismissive wave of her hand. "Let's see... Benedict, Darcy, Zachary... I think one was called Michael—what's so spectacular about that? But then my favorite—Peaceful!"

Fantine closed her eyes and cringed. "Peaceful?!"

"*Oui!* Is it not astounding?"

Fantine opened her eyes to Mrs. Pettigrew's wide smile. "The poor man..."

"Nonsense, he came from a very rich family. Or at least they were at one time. But the war, you know..."

Fantine shook her head, a hand to her temple. "I am confused."

"You won't be once I tell you the story."

"But what do the girl's six brothers have to do with anything?"

"Everything!"

Fantine nodded weakly. "Of course."

Mrs. Pettigrew smiled and readjusted herself on the cushion. "This happened not long after Tom Turner returned to Clear Creek to take over as sheriff."

"And it begins here in Denver?"

"Not at all. It begins in Savannah, Georgia!"

Fantine nodded again. "Naturally."

Mrs. Pettigrew smiled. "And this, *ma cherie*, is what happened..."

Chapter One

Savannah, Georgia, early March 1877

Buford Ulysses Comfort paced his study, his heavy jowls trembling every time he turned on his heel and stomped to the other side of the room. After several moments of this he went behind his desk and spun toward his eldest son. "I don't care how long it takes you!" he bellowed in a heavy Southern accent. "Take your brothers and scour the countryside! Find her, Major, confound it, or we'll be ruined!"

Major sighed in resignation. "Perhaps if you'd found another way to get us out of our current financial difficulty, Father," he said in his own deep, smooth drawl, "my sister would not have deemed it necessary to run away."

"Ungrateful, that's what she is!" his father barked. "Haven't I given her everything she's ever wanted, bent to her every whim? And *this* is how she repays me? Now that her family needs her, she abandons us!"

"Rupert Jerney is, in my opinion, a bit of a cad—and

I would say that even if he weren't a Yankee carpet-bagger. I believe if I were Pleasant, I'd have run too."

"Well, you're not your sister, are you? And I don't care what you think of Mr. Jerney. He's our only way out of this mess and I fully plan to take him up on his offer. Now go find your sister, no matter what it takes, and bring her back! She's going to marry Rupert Jerney whether she likes it or not!"

Major put his hands behind his back and sighed again. "You do realize, of course, that you're sacrificing her happiness for your bank accounts?"

His father's lips formed into a fine line as his eyes bulged. "You're one to talk!" he exploded. "This plantation has been in our family for generations! And if you'd like to inherit it lock, stock and barrel, then I suggest you find your sister. Her sacrifice is going to save us all!"

"Except her," Major pointed out.

"Get going!" his father shouted. "I will not lose Comfort Fields!"

Major took one last look at his father's flustered face, shook his head, turned and headed for the door. "Then may my brothers and I be forgiven for what we're about to do," he muttered. He let the door slam on his way out, ignoring the furious shouts of his father from the other side.

On the one hand, he couldn't blame him for being so upset. Comfort Fields was started by his great-grandfather and had grown into one of the biggest plantations around Savannah. But the War Between the States took its toll, not to mention the carpetbaggers and everything else that came after it to suck the life out of the once proud South.

Twelve years later, though, one would think his family would have recovered by now.

But no. The Comfort family, Major had recently come to find out, was deep in debt. Buford wasn't the best at managing the plantation's money—that had been their mother's area of expertise. Even as eccentric as Olympia Comfort had been, she still mastered the plantation's books like a fine artist, not to mention being a superb hostess and incredibly kindhearted. Her gifts helped balance some of her eccentricities, such as her penchant for bestowing upon some of her children her ideas of distinguished names.

Major shuddered at the thought and continued to the drawing room where his brothers waited.

He had been the first to suffer her creative mind by being dubbed Major Quincy Comfort. Only his father called him Major, his siblings mercifully referred to him as Quince. There was nothing wrong with the name Major—it had been rather fashionable at the time—but when coupled with his surname…needless to say, he'd learned how to use his fists at a tender age. She'd given more normal names to others of his siblings. Michael John was the second son, followed by Darcy Jefferson (okay, so she was reading Jane Austen novels while she carried him) and Zachary Nathaniel and Benedict Andrew.

And then, disaster. Mother died giving birth to the youngest siblings, the twins. Before she passed, she'd chosen their names, and their heartbroken father hadn't been able to refuse her last wish. She'd told him to raise them to be pleasant and peaceful children. Thus they became Pleasant Anne and Peaceful Mathias Comfort. Pleasant was just called Pleasant, as her brothers thought Anne too boorish. Peaceful, on the other hand, was simply Matt, which in turn kept the house…well, peaceful.

But once he informed his brothers of what Pleasant had done, things might not stay that way.

Major stepped into the drawing room where his brothers—and an unexpected guest, waited. "Mr. Jerney," he said as he entered, suppressing a wince. "What a…pleasant surprise!"

Rupert Jerney, a tall, thin, conceited man, looked down his nose at him. "I see nothing pleasant about it," he said in his flat, nasal New England accent. He sniffed a few times, one of his many annoying habits. "Which is why I'm heah to begin with. Where's yaw sister? I wish to speak with her."

Major glanced at his brothers. "Our sister is otherwise engaged at the moment," he advised in his most sophisticated manner. He knew Rupert prided himself on proper decorum at all times—at least in public. "Perhaps if you'd sent word that you wished to call on her?"

"No mattah—she'll see me soon enough. Where is your fathah, then? I have business with him as well."

Major clasped his hands behind his back and raised his chin ever so slightly, a silent signal to his brothers. Darcy and Zachary's eyes began to dart between him and their guest. "He's in his study."

"Fine." Rupert headed for the drawing room's double doors. Benedict and Michael, the only two brothers sitting, stood as if to escort him. "I know the way," Rupert informed them haughtily and marched from the room.

As soon as he was gone, Michael asked, "What is it? What's happened?"

"This has to do with Pleasant, doesn't it?" Darcy added.

"Indeed it does," Major said. "For one, she's missing. Probably left sometime in the night."

"What?" several of them said in surprise.

"Quince," Benedict inquired. "Are you saying she ran away?"

"Wouldn't you if you had to marry...*that*?" he said with a toss of his head toward the doors.

"Rupert?!" the brothers said at once.

"Unfortunately for poor Pleasant, yes."

Michael stepped forward. "She can't marry Rupert!"

"Our father thinks differently and has assigned us the task of rounding her up to do so."

"Why Rupert?" Zachary asked, suspicious. "We all know she can't stand the sight of him. None of us can!"

"Nor should we," Michael added. "I've met a few honest and forthright Yankees, I admit, and several more who weren't so bad." Unconsciously, he rubbed the stumps on his right hand, where he'd lost two fingers to a Minie ball at Milledgeville. It had been a Union doctor who'd patched him up. "But Rupert Jerney would be a blackguard even if he were born and raised in Virginia. So why him?"

"Because he's rich, that's why," Major said in disgust. "His sawmills in Maine and New Hampshire didn't suffer as our plantations did. He's only grown richer in the war's aftermath, and offered to bail Father out of debt. Problem is, he wants Pleasant as collateral."

His brothers stared at him in shock. "So it's true," Benedict finally said. "Father has run Comfort Fields into the ground."

"I'm afraid he has," Major said.

"But wasn't Father grooming you to take over?" Darcy asked.

"He said he would, years ago, but he never really did," Major said. "I think perhaps he was hiding our situation in hopes of pulling us out of it before showing me how to operate things."

"Pride cometh before destruction," Zachary quoted.

"Indeed," Major agreed. "Apparently Rupert will pay off most of his debts, so long as he can have Pleasant as his wife."

"That's diabolical!" Benedict said in shock.

"I don't think it sounds so bad," Matt put in.

His brothers looked at him, aghast. "And if it were *you* that had to marry Rupert, how happy would you be about it?" Michael asked.

"Well…yes, I see your point." Matt glanced at the double doors of the drawing room, then back at his brothers. "Maybe he's nicer at home."

"From what I've heard, quite the opposite," Benedict said. "But then, what else can we do? We'll lose everything."

"Right you are," Major agreed. He eyed them, his face an expressionless mask. "So do we sacrifice our sister's happiness to continue in the life we've grown accustomed to, or do we stand by her side and refuse Rupert's—as Benedict put it—'diabolical' offer?"

His brothers stared at him as they thought on their answer. It didn't take them long to decide.

Denver, Colorado, later that same month…

"But, Aunt Phidelia," Pleasant begged, "why can't you listen to reason?"

"Because there *is* no reason to this madness! Your father has clearly gone 'round the bend, my dear, and lost all his mental faculties. I haven't the faintest idea why he would write such an outlandish letter and demand I send word to him the moment I see you. Of course I haven't. I won't stand by and see you marry that sniveling Yankee weasel Rupert Travel!"

"Jerney," Pleasant corrected with a grimace.

"Even worse!"

"Yes, I know," she agreed. It was bad enough her Christian name was Pleasant Comfort—to become Pleasant Jerney would be too much to bear. It was one of the reasons she'd run away in the first place. The only place to go was Denver to see Aunt Phidelia. Her mother's sister was a kindly soul who would be willing to help Pleasant escape her current circumstances.

"You realize, of course, he'll send *them* after you."

"Them?"

"Your brothers, you silly girl, who else?"

Pleasant paced to the other side of the parlor and back. "Oh yes. *Them*." She turned to her aunt. "Major, most likely. I can't see the others coming with him."

"With what's left of your family's fortune draining away? Trust me, my dear, they most certainly will. And they'll drag you back and use you to keep Comfort Fields going."

Pleasant cocked her head to the side, the action sending a dark, loose curl across her face. "How do you know all of this?"

"Because your father wrote it in his letter!" Aunt Phidelia said, waving the missive in the air. "Your only hope is to keep going. You can't stay here."

Pleasant's eyes misted with tears. "But, Auntie, where will I go? We haven't any relatives west of here!"

"True, we don't," she said solemnly. "Which means we'll have to resort to drastic measures."

Pleasant paled. "What sort of drastic measures?"

Her aunt narrowed her eyes. "You'll have to learn how to work!"

Pleasant fell into the nearest chair. "No!"

"Yes!"

Pleasant gripped the chair's arms. She'd never worked a day in her life in any conventional sense. She was just a little girl when the War Between the States broke out, and an admittedly spoiled one at that. But after she'd witnessed the cruel suffering of others, the "comforts" of bearing the Comfort name didn't mean much anymore. People had died all around her, and her father, God bless him, had done all he could to shelter her from that horrible storm.

But this was something else entirely. He might as well march her out in front of a Grand Army firing squad and give the command to shoot her himself! Rupert Jerney, indeed.

"There is another solution," her aunt continued. "You'll still have to work, but at least it would be in the domestic realm."

Pleasant stared, her mouth half-open in shock. She was still getting over her aunt's earlier revelation. "What?"

"Pay a visit to Adelia Pettigrew."

Pleasant straightened in her chair, a puzzled look on her face. "Who is Adelia Pettigrew?"

"She runs a mail-order bride agency in town. I wouldn't suggest her at all, seeing as how she's a…well, a crackpot. But desperate times call for desperate measures. I do hear all her brides are blissfully married."

"Blissfully?" Pleasant said, a hint of hope in her voice.

"Indeed. We'll pay her a visit first thing in the morning. If we're lucky, she'll have a nice Southern groom wanting a wife someplace like California—that's about as far from here as you can get!"

"But, Auntie…marry a complete stranger?"

"It's a complete stranger or Rupert Jerney. Which would you prefer?"

Pleasant looked at her hands. They were creamy and smooth, the skin soft to the touch. If she married Rupert, she'd not want for any material thing, but she'd be stuck in a loveless marriage with a man she didn't like to begin with. Set aside that he was a Yankee—there were good Yankees, she knew. But Rupert wasn't one of them. He liked to boast, was a complete boor, thought himself better than everyone else and reportedly had more than a passing interest in the bawdy houses. So what if he was rich? Money did not make the man.

She glanced at her hands again. Better to marry a stranger and pray he was kind than risk a life with Rupert. True, she might have rough, dry hands with a stranger, but if he was kind and of good moral character, how much did that matter?

Speaking of matter… "Auntie, what about Comfort Fields?"

"What about it? Your father has nothing left to keep it going. From the sounds of it, the banks are going to take it if he doesn't pay his debts. And they will, mark my words. But your brothers are all talented enough. They'll get along."

"And Papa?"

Phidelia sighed wearily. "I suspect he'll come here to live with me."

Pleasant stood. "I can't ask you to do—"

"It's no trouble, child. I've always enjoyed his company—when he wasn't being an unreasonable goat, that is. Right now he's beyond reason."

"But my brothers' inheritance…"

"…was lost by your father a long time ago. The war more than anything took it from them. All your father has done these last few years is forestall the inevitable."

"But what will they do? Where will they go?"

"They're a resourceful bunch, my dear—they won't be completely penniless. You're the one that will be in the long run. You've got to marry!"

Her aunt was right, of course. There was no help for it. If she didn't marry and fast, she'd be forced by Father to wed Rupert. Pleasant massaged her temples a moment, eyes closed. When she opened them, she said, "Very well, Mrs. Pettigrew it is."

Mrs. Pettigrew tapped her fingers on her desk as she looked Pleasant up and down. Aunt Phidelia sat nervously in a chair off to one side, as if expecting the finely carved piece of furniture to explode at any moment.

Pleasant stood before the desk, still as a statue. "Well?"

Mrs. Pettigrew met her gaze. "Well what, *ma cherie*?" She had been throwing around French phrases all morning. Pleasant had initially thought she might be from Louisiana, but no, the accent wasn't right…

"Are you going to sit there and stare at me all day, or are we to get down to business?"

Mrs. Pettigrew arched an eyebrow. "What a lovely accent you have, *ma belle*." She looked at her aunt. "Speaks her mind, doesn't she?"

"She always has," Aunt Phidelia agreed.

"Hmmm," Mrs. Pettigrew mused as she went back to studying the prospective bride.

Pleasant fought the urge to roll her eyes in impatience. It wouldn't do to upset the woman. Her reputation for perfect matches surprised even Pleasant. In the year Mrs. Pettigrew had been in business, she'd sent out dozens of brides, all of which, according to Mrs. Pettigrew herself, were now happily married.

If that weren't enough, the writing to prove it was on the wall. Literally—Mrs. Pettigrew had taken to displaying the letters she'd received from her happy customers on the wall behind her desk. A perusal of them had convinced Pleasant and her aunt they'd made the right choice in coming. But was Mrs. Pettigrew as impressed with them as they were with her? The way she was looking at Pleasant made her feel as though she was about to be dismissed without a second thought.

"Well," Mrs. Pettigrew finally said. "I believe I have a gentleman that will be able to handle you."

Pleasant's eyes bulged. "What? *Handle* me?!"

Mrs. Pettigrew didn't bat an eye. Instead she pulled out a drawer of her desk and extracted a few sheets of paper. "You'll want to write him while you're here and let him know you've accepted his proposal."

"Proposal? You haven't so much as shown me a letter!"

"Oh, *ça va*." Mrs. Pettigrew smiled, removed one sheet and shoved it across the desk. "Here is *Monsieur* Turner's proposal."

Aunt Phidelia cleared her throat. "Er, isn't it customary they write to one another first, to see if they suit?"

"Considering your situation, I wouldn't think there was time. This particular gentleman seeks a wife now. He isn't looking for lengthy letter-writing."

Aunt Phidelia gasped. "We've not said a word about our situation. How would you know...?"

"By the way you're fidgeting about in your chair, *Madame*." She looked at Pleasant. "And this one—she stands rigid, with no hope of love in her eyes."

Pleasant exchanged a quick glance with her aunt. Good grief, did they really look that desperate?

"I suggest that if you're in a hurry, you read *Monsieur* Turner's proposal," Mrs. Pettigrew said, drawing her attention.

Pleasant's mouth dropped open. "How did you... I mean..." She straightened. "How dare you insinuate that I may be guilty of..."

"I insinuate nothing. I know only that you are acting in haste, and therefore must have reason. I am not worried about why—that is entirely your affair. *My* affair is to help speed you on your way." She gave the letter another shove. "Read, *s'il vous plaît*."

Pleasant looked at Aunt Phidelia, who shrugged. If Mrs. Pettigrew wasn't concerned with the whys and wherefores, so much the better. She swallowed hard, steeled her nerves and picked up the letter.

Chapter Two

To my future bride:

My name is Eli Turner. I am writing to tell you how much I look forward to meeting you. I am a stable man with a stable job. I have a small cabin outside of town that I am sure you will find most comfortable. Clear Creek is a wonderful place with plenty of fresh air and perpetual beauty. I do not know you yet, but I will. On the recommendation of one of my closest friends, Sheriff Harlan Hughes, not to mention one of my relations, I am putting my full trust in Mrs. Pettigrew to find you for me.

I am tall with brown hair and hazel eyes. You will find me an amiable man capable of decent conversation. I require a wife who can cook, clean and sew, but that goes without saying.

In closing, will you be my bride? If so, I have enclosed train and stage fare and look forward to meeting you in person when you arrive.

Sincerely yours,
Eli Turner

Pleasant looked up from the letter nervously. "What does *decent conversation* mean, exactly?"

"What do you mean? What did he say?" Aunt Phidelia asked as she stood. She went to her, peered over her shoulder at the letter and quickly read it. "That is a rather odd phrase. What sort of man is this?"

"One that can deal with *Mademoiselle* Comfort here," Mrs. Pettigrew said dryly. "You can either accept or reject his proposal."

Pleasant's face twisted with indecision as she stared at Mrs. Pettigrew. "And this man trusts you to choose a bride for him? Does not the bride choose the husband?"

"You'll find me quite adept at what I do, *Mademoiselle* Comfort."

"I… I… Oh, what if he's a gentleman of four outs?" Pleasant had heard some of her friends in Savannah describe undesirable men that way—being without money, without wit, without credit and without manners.

Mrs. Pettigrew smiled. "Does his letter not state that he has a steady job? Therefore he must have money. And look at what he writes! He has a mind, this one, and manners. He is not some witless stump. As to his credit, I cannot say. Clear Creek is a small town, as I understand it—who knows if the mercantile there gives credit or not? So." The woman tapped her nails against the desk. "Are you interested in this man or not?"

"Is he the only applicant you have?" asked Aunt Phidelia.

"He is the only applicant I have for *Mademoiselle* Comfort. The others will not do."

"And may I ask why not?" Pleasant inquired, her tone bordering on haughtiness.

Mrs. Pettigrew placed a silver monocle over one eye and studied her a moment. "Because you are not suited to them."

Now she did get haughty. "Who are you to tell me if they will suit or not?"

"Pleasant, dear," Aunt Phidelia said in warning. "If Mrs. Pettigrew says this Mr. Turner is the best choice, then I don't think we should argue."

Mrs. Pettigrew let the monocle fall from her eye. It was attached to her dress by a silver chain. Pleasant noticed a tiny pocket had been sewn into the woman's dress for it—she noticed when Mrs. Pettigrew made use of it and placed the monocle inside. "Mr. Turner is your best chance of escaping…whatever it is you need to escape from."

Pleasant sighed. "Very well. My brothers aren't likely to follow me across the country."

"Ah," Mrs. Pettigrew said. "How many brothers?"

"Six," she said flatly.

"*Sacre bleu!*" Mrs. Pettigrew said. "Let us hope you are right, for it would not bode well for your brothers should they follow you as far as Clear Creek."

"Why is that?" Aunt Phidelia asked.

"I have heard that the residents there are very…close-knit. In other words, your brothers wouldn't be taking on just one man, but the entire town. And the man I'm sending you to is the brother of the local sheriff, a man of some renown. At least in the Far West."

"Does *he* need a wife?" Aunt Phidelia asked.

"No, he already has one. One of the brides I sent out last year wrote to tell me she had the pleasure of meeting the couple. She has since come to know them quite well. I trust *Mademoiselle* Comfort will too."

Pleasant spied a nearby chair and sat in resignation. "Very well. Where do I sign?"

"Not sign, *ma cherie*. Write. Tell him you are coming. A few words about yourself would be advisable."

Pleasant couldn't believe it. She felt her jaw shake in her effort to hold back tears. This was it. She'd be leaving her beloved Georgia forever to marry some stranger out West! And all because her father got some notion in his head that Rupert would bail him out of his debt if he married her. Ha! She knew Rupert—he'd never do it. Once he had her he'd probably sit back and *enjoy* watching the last of her father's legacy crumble into ruin. If only Father would listen to reason. But a desperate man rarely listened to anyone once his eyes were set on what he thought was a solution.

"Fine," she said at last. "I'll write him a note. When should I say I'm leaving?"

Mrs. Pettigrew thought a moment. "Considering your current circumstances, is tomorrow too soon?"

Clear Creek, Oregon, three weeks later

Dear Mr. Turner,

I have read your letter and accept your proposal of marriage. By the time you read this I will be well on my way to Clear Creek. I should arrive on the stage Friday, April 13 at noon. I will endeavor to make you a good wife. I trust you will do the same as a husband.

Sincerely,
Miss P.A. Comfort

"That's it?" Sheriff Tom Turner asked, scratching his head. "She didn't say nothin' else?"

"Nope." Eli turned the letter over to check if anything was written on the back. "That was it."

"Strange, don't ya think? She didn't even describe herself."

Eli blanched. "Tarnation, yer right! Ya think that's a bad sign?"

Tom stared at the letter a moment. "Ya described *yer* looks…well, Colin Cooke did anyways."

"Maybe I shoulda wrote that letter myself. But ya know how bad I spell and all."

Tom nodded. "Yeah, I know. She might not be too happy to find out yer not as, whatcha say…*eloquent* in person."

Eli took off his hat and ran a hand through his brown hair. "What am I gonna do, Tom? Maybe she read Colin's fancy talk in that letter and jumped at the chance to be with a real country-gentleman-type fella."

"But ya are a country-gentleman type."

Eli held his hands out from his sides. "No, I ain't— look at me! Country, sure, but Colin and Harrison done explained to me what it means to be a gentleman in England and I ain't *that*!"

"Of course not. We're not in England."

"Oh, ya know what I mean. I ain't nothin' but a lowly deputy workin' for my older brother."

Tom sighed and put an arm around him. "Yer a fine deputy, workin' for a sheriff that sorely needs yer help."

"Ya already had Bran O'Hare and Henry Fig helpin' ya. I dunno why ya hired me on too—unless ya felt sorry for me."

"I hired ya on 'cause Henry's gettin' ready to retire. He'll be gone soon, ya know that—and he don't get around so fast even when he's here, what with his lumbago."

Eli rolled his eyes and smacked his forehead. "Dog-gone it! This whole mail-order bride business has me more addled than I thought—I plumb forgot about Henry retirin'! Maybe sendin' away for one wasn't such a good idea."

Tom chuckled. "Eli, yer twenty-six years old. It's high time ya got married. You'd already be hitched if'n ya took my advice and gone for Honoria Cooke."

"Honoria? No way—she scares me!"

Tom placed his hands on his hips. "Scares ya? What for?"

"She's…well she's…opinionated. And once she gets started on a subject and thinks she's right, she goes until she proves it! Besides, I don't think I could handle havin' Harrison as a father-in-law. I feel sorry for the poor fella ends up with her."

"Well, no chance of that happenin' anytime soon. Ain't no one else 'round here for her to court."

Eli shrugged. "She just ain't the right girl for me, that's all. You of all people should know 'bout that."

Tom's mouth formed into a firm line as he nodded. He'd gotten as far as the altar with the wrong bride—only by his own fortitude, and that of Matty Quinn, did he end up with the right one. "How I ended up married to Rose took some guts. Like not givin' in to what everyone in town says about ya marryin' Honoria—that took guts too. Ya did the right thing sendin' away for a bride, brother."

"Maybe so, but my bride not puttin' no description

of herself in that letter still makes me nervous. What if she's hard on the eyes?"

Tom blew out a breath. "Then I guess ya take the time to see if'n ya like the rest of her better."

"But the way Colin wrote that letter, I proposed right away. She's comin' here 'spectin' to marry me right off, not court first."

"Who says ya gotta?"

Eli opened his mouth to speak then shut it. His brother was right—he didn't *have* to marry the girl right away. He ought to court her a little, just to make sure. But then what if he decided he didn't like her, hard on the eyes or not? Worse, what if she wasn't bad on the eyes, but was on the temperament? If she was beyond beautiful, he might die trying to get past a bad temper, like beating his head against the woodpile over and over and...

"You okay?" Tom asked.

Eli nodded. "Yeah, just thinkin'."

"Well, best not think too long," Tom said. "Friday's just a few days off."

"What?" Eli said in shock. He looked at the calendar on the wall, then rolled his eyes and looked at his brother. "Friday the 13th. Figgers. I'm telling ya, this was a bad idea."

"And I'm tellin' ya I think it was a great one. Now stop fussin' and make yerself a list of things ya need to get done. Yer Sunday best need ironin'?"

"No, I got 'em hangin' up at home."

"Good, that's one less thing ya have to do. Is the house clean?"

"Well, it could do with a good dustin'."

"Eli, why ain't ya takin' care of this?"

He shrugged. "Just didn't think of it, I guess. I've had other things on my mind."

"Like what?"

Eli's mouth twisted up into a lopsided smile. "Like if'n I'm really the marryin' kind."

"'Course ya are—what man ain't?"

"Look at Sheriff Hughes—he was a bachelor for years. Decades."

"Was," Tom pointed out. He put his hands on his hips again. "Ya ain't scared, are ya?"

"Me, scared? I ain't afraid of no woman!" He looked away and mumbled, "Except maybe Honoria."

"Good—then ask our sister Emeline to help ya clean up that sorry excuse of a cabin of yers. Heck, I bet Lena Adams might help—she ain't far from yer place. She could bring her sister Fina."

Eli nodded. Even though his cabin was built only a couple of years ago, it wasn't the most organized. He didn't concern himself with housecleaning—he was the only one living there, and he didn't care how it looked. "Fine, I'll ask Emeline and Mrs. Adams if they'll help."

"I'll tell Rose—she can pitch in too," Tom said. "Between the three of 'em, yer place ought to be shipshape by the time yer bride arrives."

Eli glanced at the calendar again. It was Tuesday the 10th. If the women started tomorrow that would give them two days. Land sakes, would they really need that much time? He wasn't that messy, was he?

"Eli Turner, this house is a pigsty!" his older sister Emeline said in disgust. "Ya'd think Ma never taught ya to pick up after yerself!"

It was early Wednesday morning and Eli didn't have

time for this—he needed to get to work. "I sleep and eat here, Emeline. I don't pay much attention to what happens in between with the place."

"One more reason ya need a wife, brother. Never have I seen such a mess." She shook her head in pity. "It's a good thing Ma ain't here to see this."

Eli sighed and nodded. Unable to farm anymore due to their age, their parents had moved to Oregon City the year before, leaving the farm to Tom and Rose. Of course, with Tom being sheriff there wasn't much farming going on, so he'd leased the land to Harvey Brown and sent the money to his parents. The arrangement worked for all involved, especially now. "She'd prob'ly box my ears," he said.

"Don't think I won't!" Emeline huffed. "It's a good thing Anson or his brothers ain't been by. You know how particular Oscar is."

Eli laughed. His sister had married Anson White, the youngest of the White brothers who ran the stage stop halfway between Clear Creek and Oregon City. Anson was a wonderful man, and Eli and Tom couldn't be happier he'd married their sister. His brothers, on the other hand, were a little odd, but they loved them and considered them part of the family.

Oscar, however, could be pretty persnickety when it came to disorganization. He liked everything in its place and for things to be neat and orderly. "Your brother-in-law'd prob'ly wanna hang me," he said with a grin.

"It ain't funny," she shot back. "He'd likely faint first."

Eli laughed louder. "I gotta get to work, Emeline. I'm sorry the place is such a mess. I guess I'm gonna have to mend my ways when it comes to straightening things up."

"That'll mainly be yer wife's job. But ya don't wanna frighten her away as soon as she gets here, do ya?"

"No, I guess not." He grabbed his hat off a peg and put it on. "I 'spect Fina and Lena'll be by any time to help. I ain't sure when Rose is comin'. Good luck."

His sister glanced around the small cabin. "Thanks, we're gonna need it."

Eli went outside and mounted his horse. He was suddenly glad he had neighbors like Lena Adams and Fina Stone, not to mention a good family. It would make his new bride happy to have friends and acquaintances nearby. He'd purchased the small piece of land from Fina's husband Levi several years ago, so his cabin sat in between the Stones' and the Adams'.

Lena and Fina and their sister Apple (who was married to Brandon O'Hare) were cousins of the Cookes who'd come to Clear Creek as mail-order brides late in the summer of 1861, all the way from England. They weren't the only ones—three of their other female cousins had arrived just over two months before to get married too. It was all the doing of Harrison and Colin Cooke's older brother Duncan, who'd inherited an honest-to-God English duchy in '59.

Eli was only a boy at the time, and couldn't have cared less about such things. For a while, he kept calling Duncan Cooke a duck instead of a duke—it took him years to get that straight. He laughed out loud to himself as he kicked his horse into a trot and headed to work.

When he got there, Tom was hanging up wanted posters on the wall. "Howdy, little brother. Is the cleaning cavalry at yer house?"

Eli looked pained. "Yep—and their captain, our lovely sister, wasn't too happy with it."

Tom turned to look at him. "That bad, huh?"

"Worse, accordin' to her."

Tom laughed. "That'll teach ya to straighten up. Emeline won't let ya forget neither. Ya better hope yer wife ain't nothin' like her—or Oscar."

"Emeline said somethin' like that too. Maybe I shoulda had *him* come over and clean. Least then it'd only be one person on my back."

Tom tacked the last poster on the wall then sat at his desk. "One look at yer place might give poor Oscar a heart attack. Then what would his wife do?"

"I count it a blessin' they live at the stage stop and not in Clear Creek. Seein' as how they just come for visits, I think I'm safe. I don't expect 'em again for a while."

"No, but one of us may have to ride out to their place and check on things." He pointed toward the three new wanted posters behind him.

"What for?" Eli grabbed a chair, brought it to the desk and sat.

Tom turned. "'Cause of that fella, the one with the bushy beard. Goes by the name of 'Lizard' Grunsky."

"Lizard? What kinda name is that?"

Tom smiled. "Oh, that ain't nothin'. His two friends on the wall next to him go by 'Snake' and 'Frog'."

Eli grimaced. "Can't these outlaws come up with better nicknames than that? Maybe they ought to talk to Cutty and Imogene. At least they name their villains somethin' decent."

Tom laughed. "That's 'cause Cutty and Imogene are the creative type. Ya read their latest?"

"Nah, is it out already?"

Tom turned to his desk drawer, pulled out a dime novel and shoved it across to him. Imogene Sayer, cousin to Lena, Fina and Apple, had married Cutty Holmes, another distant cousin of the Cookes. Together they penned adventure stories under the name "C. I. Sayer." They were growing in popularity too, and now had a publisher in San Francisco that wanted to compile their stories into a large book. "I read it last night. It's their best yet."

Eli smiled as he picked up the small book and flipped through the pages. "I'll read it later." He looked at Tom. "Ya know I cain't go out to the Whites', not with my bride comin' to town Friday. I ain't got the time."

"I know—that's why I'm sendin' Bran. Willie thought he saw some men camped near the road between here and the Whites' a few days ago when he drove the stage through. Best to warn 'em in case there's any trouble nearby."

Eli nodded his agreement. Trouble. First a new bride, and now this. What trouble, he wondered, would Friday bring?

Chapter Three

"Clear Creek! Comin' inna Clear Creek!" Willie the stage driver yelled as they pulled into the tiny town. The only reason Pleasant knew his name was that he'd introduced himself to everyone at the previous stage stop whether they were heading to Clear Creek or not. Lanky of build, a little shy and missing his two front teeth, he was the most personable driver she'd ever met.

And to be honest, she was traveling alone, and knowing the fellow's name put her more at ease. Maybe that was the point of his introductions—either that, or he really was a friendly sort.

Willie brought the stage to a stop in front of a two-story building with a huge sign on the front: "DUNNIGAN'S MERCANTILE". It was a pretty place, with two huge windows on either side of the windowed double doors. It would be light and bright inside, something she liked. She wondered what sort of goods they sold—would they have anything like what she'd find in a store in the South, or would there be nothing at all?

That pointed to a larger question: just how wild was this "Wild West" she'd heard about? All she knew was what she'd gleaned from the dime novels Darcy and Michael read and talked about all the time. Silly boys—they'd even managed to suck Benedict and Matt into them. She abhorred them and had never read one herself, figuring they were all a bunch of nonsense. But… were they?

The stage door opened to Willie's wide grin. She did her best not to giggle at his missing teeth and took the hand he offered. She was here and that was all that mattered. She would now survive, albeit as the wife of a stranger. But she had convinced herself during her long journey that she would make the same decision no matter what, because she simply could not marry Rupert! The die was cast.

Pleasant disembarked and glanced around as Willie climbed back onto the stage to retrieve her trunk and satchel. She'd brought only the bare necessities—for a well-bred Southern belle, traveling with one trunk and one satchel was horrifyingly sparse indeed. But, she was determined she would manage.

The doors to the mercantile opened, drawing her attention. An older man with white hair and a mustache and wearing an apron emerged onto the porch, hooked his thumbs in his suspenders and smiled. "Howdy," he called out to her. "You must be Eli Turner's mail-order bride."

She nodded. "You are correct, sir," she said politely. She glanced this way and that. This appeared to be the main street of the town—and perhaps the only street. Only time would tell about that. "May I inquire as to where Mr. Turner is at present?"

The man smiled again. "Hain't the slightest idea,

ma'am. But you're welcome to come inside and wait for him."

Pleasant's back went rigid. Here she'd traveled all this way, and her groom didn't even have the decency to meet her? "I hope he has a good excuse," she muttered to herself.

Willie carried her trunk up the porch steps and set it down next to the older gentleman. "Howdy, Wilfred!" he greeted. "Looks like Eli done got hisself a right purty bride, don't he? She talks purty too."

Wilfred looked her up and down as she ascended the mercantile steps. "He sure did. About time we had another wedding around here—it's been awhile."

"Yer right 'bout that," Willie agreed.

Pleasant was starting to get irritated. "If you two gentlemen are done discussing my nuptials, could you please tell me where Mr. Turner is?"

"Done already told you," Wilfred said. "Come inside and have a licorice whip while you wait. Maybe a cup of tea?"

Pleasant smiled. Did he just offer her tea? Perhaps they hadn't meant to be rude, talking about her as if she hadn't been there. Hopefully the whole town was at least this friendly. "Thank you, I'd like a cup of tea."

"Right this way, miss." Wilfred turned around and opened the door for her. Pleasant lifted her skirts and entered the building.

It was just as charming inside as out, and more bright and airy than she'd expected. The high ceiling and white interior lifted her spirits, and the many-colored goods lining the shelves helped. She'd seen so many dark, dreary places on her journey that she'd despaired of seeing beauty again. At least inside—some of the countryside was spectacular, but she wasn't going to live on a mountain peak next to a giant pine, was she?

A stocky woman with salt-and-pepper hair came out from behind a curtained doorway and waddled behind the front counter. "Wilfred, what are you doing?" she barked. "We have inventory!"

"Yes, Irene, I know." He turned to Pleasant. "But first I'd like to introduce you to Eli's future bride."

The woman squinted, then reached into her apron pocket, pulled out a pair of spectacles and put them on. "Oh. I see."

Pleasant tried not to smile. Obviously the woman couldn't manage without them. "How do you do?" she replied with a curtsy.

"Land sakes, a foreigner!" the woman barked.

"She ain't no furriner, Mrs. Dunnigan," said Willie. "But she did come all the way from Coloradah."

"Colorado? I had no idea they talked like that there." Mrs. Dunnigan studied Pleasant.

"I traveled from Colorado," Pleasant informed them. "But I hail from Savannah, Georgia."

"Georgia?" Wilfred said. "Oh, that ain't that far. We got folks around here from a lot farther away than that!"

Pleasant arched an eyebrow at him. "Really?"

"Oh yeah." Wilfred went to the counter. "Irene, get this woman a licorice whip while I run upstairs and fetch her a cup of tea."

"Tea?" the woman barked. "What does she need tea for? Where's Eli?"

Wilfred shrugged. "Working."

"Working? The day his bride comes to town? What kind of an imbecile is he?"

Pleasant couldn't hide her smile. She was beginning

to like this woman despite her crassness. Between her attitude and her accent, Irene Dunnigan reminded her of certain matrons back home—tough women who'd kept their families together and fed through the war through sheer stubbornness.

Wilfred whispered into Irene's ear, and her eyes went wide. "Oh. I see. Well then."

"Is there something I should know?" Pleasant asked.

"No!" Irene barked. "Come here and get your candy!"

Pleasant's feet were moving before she had time to think. Yes, clearly this woman was used to being in command. A few more generals like her, and maybe the South would've won. She looked at Wilfred. "I take it you're Mr. Dunnigan?"

"Yes, ma'am—all my life."

Irene—Wilfred's wife, presumably—smacked him on the arm. "Wilfred, get the woman her tea!" He smiled good-naturedly, turned on his heel and disappeared behind the curtained doorway.

Pleasant listened as he hurried up a set of unseen stairs that must lead to their living quarters above, then turned back to Mrs. Dunnigan. "Is something wrong with Mr. Turner?"

Mrs. Dunnigan stuffed a few pieces of candy into a little white paper bag. "No, but he's taking care of official business. Never bother a lawman when he's on duty—that's something you'd best learn now if you're gonna marry the man."

Pleasant gulped before she could stop herself. "Are there…many outlaws around here?"

"Plenty lately. It's getting so a person can't travel across the prairie anymore by themselves. Blasted curs are bad for business!" She tossed in the last piece, twisted the bag shut and handed it to her. "Here!"

Pleasant jumped at her loud voice, reached out and took it. She'd never allowed anyone to speak to her in such a manner back home. But she wasn't back home. This was where she would live now, and she had to get used to these people and their ways.

Mr. Dunnigan came downstairs and emerged through the curtained doorway, a cup of tea in his hands. "Here ya go, Miss… I don't think we caught your name."

"My apologies—I forgot to give it. I'm Miss Comfort."

The Dunnigans exchanged a quick glance. "Pleased to make your acquaintance," Mr. Dunnigan said. "You can sit in here as long as you like. There's a table and chairs over by the window."

Pleasant turned and, sure enough, there was a lovely little table and two chairs. "What a nice spot." She turned to Mrs. Dunnigan. "Do you take tea there?"

"Nope," Mrs. Dunnigan informed her with a scowl. "That's the men's checker table."

"Oh." Pleasant walked over to it. A checkerboard had been painted onto its surface. "So it is." She set down her teacup then studied the mercantile. "Is this the only store in town?"

"Of course it is!" Mrs. Dunnigan snapped. "You don't think this town is big enough for two, do you?"

"Now, Irene, how could she know?" Wilfred countered. "She just got here."

Pleasant gave them a half-smile. "How many people live in Clear Creek?" She was almost afraid of the answer.

"Let's see," Wilfred mused. "Must be close to a hundred by now. Town's been growing by leaps and bounds the last twelve years or so on account of all the young-guns folks keep having."

"You mean children?" Pleasant asked.

"That's what he said, isn't it?" his wife barked.

Pleasant gave a slow nod. "Of course. How silly of me." Egads, was Mrs. Dunnigan offended by everything?

Before she could think about it further, the doors opened to two extremely handsome men, much older than her—both had a touch of grey at the temples. Otherwise, one had sable-brown hair and dark eyes; the other a dark blonde, his eyes hazel. Despite those differences, they had similar enough features to clearly be related.

"Wilfred," the dark-haired one called in—could it be?—*a British accent.* Then he smiled at Pleasant. "We've come for the young lady."

Pleasant stood. They made her sound like a package they were picking up. "You've what?"

The other one approached and bowed. "Colin Cooke, at your service, ma'am. This is my brother Harrison. Mr. Turner has sent us to fetch you for him."

"Fetch me? Where is Mr. Turner?"

The two men exchanged a look. "He is…otherwise engaged at the moment," Harrison said. "Allow us to escort you to the hotel—or if you prefer, you may dine with us at the Triple-C and we'll deliver you to the hotel later this evening."

Pleasant stared at them, not knowing what to think. What in heaven's name did *otherwise engaged* entail? "I demand to know where Mr. Turner is."

Another look exchanged. "Perhaps it would be better if he told you himself once he returns to town," Colin said.

Pleasant shook herself. Obviously they were not going to be forthcoming. "Mr. Turner aside, may I inquire as to where you are from, sirs?"

"Sussex, England originally," said Harrison.

"And most recently, Mulligan's Saloon," Colin added cheerfully. Harrison rolled his eyes.

Pleasant was tempted to do the same. "Am I to understand that you two gentlemen have been drinking?"

"No, nothing of the kind," Harrison assured her. "We were helping Mr. Mulligan fix his back porch steps. We saw he needed some help, so we pitched in."

Pleasant took a deep breath. "Forgive me for insinuating that…"

"Not at all," Colin replied. "A perfectly reasonable assumption, Miss…?"

"Comfort."

The two smiled at each other. "Miss Comfort, the hotel or the ranch?" Harrison asked. "Which would you prefer?"

"The ranch of course!" Mrs. Dunnigan barked. "How would you like to be in a strange place sitting up in a hotel room with no one to talk to?"

"Well said," Colin agreed. "The ranch it is."

"But… I don't think…" Pleasant began.

"Nonsense," Harrison said. "You'll love meeting our wives, and they love regaling people with tales of…well, hopefully they'll contain themselves."

"Yes, we wouldn't want them scaring you on your first day in town," Colin quipped as he offered her his arm. "Shall we, then?"

She couldn't argue with their manners, but… "What about Mr. Turner?"

"He'll be along as soon as he and his brother, the sheriff, lock up the current crew of miscreants," Colin said cheerfully.

"Outlaws?!"

"Now, now—you've naught to worry about," Harrison consoled, then winked at Wilfred.

The older man's eyes popped. He went behind the counter, produced a shotgun and cocked it, then nodded back.

Pleasant felt as if she might faint. "What's going on?"

"As my brother said, there's no need to worry. Your future husband is a crack shot."

"Crack shot?" she squeaked. "What's he shooting at?"

"The outlaws, of course," Harrison answered. "Now let's be on our way, shall we?"

A loud bang caught everyone's attention. They turned to the counter where Mrs. Dunnigan had produced a hatchet and banged it on the counter. "Good heavens!" Pleasant yelped in alarm.

"No dirty outlaw is gonna come in here and steal any of our goods!" Mrs. Dunnigan huffed.

Pleasant, a hand to her chest, stared at the older couple now ready for action. What kind of a town was this? Was the outlaw problem really that bad? And what about Mr. Turner? Would there even *be* a Mr. Turner when the night was done?

"I say Miss Comfort, you're not looking very well," Colin said with concern. "The sooner we get you to the ranch the better, I think."

"B-b-b-but is it safe?" she asked. "If there are outlaws running around, how are we to get to your ranch?"

"Not to worry," Harrison said. "All the shooting is at least several miles in the opposite direction of our place."

"Shooting!" she gasped. "As in, they're shooting at *each other*?"

"Of course," Colin quipped as he reached for her trunk. "If an outlaw were to shoot at me, I'd most certainly shoot back. And I have."

Pleasant felt her knees go weak. "Please be so kind as to get me out of this town."

"Certainly," Harrison said and deftly snatched up her satchel. He tipped his hat to the Dunnigans, who still stood behind the counter, armed and ready. "Wilfred, Irene. Good day to you."

Mrs. Dunnigan banged her hatchet on the counter again. "And to you!"

Pleasant cringed as she was escorted out the double doors of the mercantile and into the street. With a man on either side of her, she felt more a prisoner. It made her nervous and she picked up her pace.

"Here now, slow down before you trip over your own feet," Colin advised. "What's your hurry? There's nothing to worry about."

"You tell me there's a band of outlaws shooting at my future husband and you expect me not to be worried?"

Colin and Harrison both looked at her, aghast. "We said no such thing!" Harrison told her.

"Quite so," Colin added. "We merely invited you to dinner."

She gaped at them. "Maybe so, but you did it while my future husband is being shot at!"

"Well, if you don't mind my saying so, he *is* the deputy sheriff," Harrison pointed out. "One of them anyway. He's bound to get shot at on occasion. Part of the job description."

"Among other things," Colin said. He steered her toward a wagon parked down the street. "I think what you need is a good hot bath, a meal and a warm bed."

"Yes, I quite agree," said his brother. "That should set you to rights. Our wives will take care of everything."

"It's a wonder you're both married!" Pleasant said. She knew she'd just insulted them, but at the moment was too flustered to care. And she couldn't help but hear gunshots somewhere in the distance. Would she be made a widow before she even had a chance to be a bride? Good grief, she'd be stranded, at least until she had Aunt Phidelia send her some money. But then what?

"Allow me to help you up," one of them offered. At this point she wasn't sure which. They both sounded alike to her.

"Miss Comfort?" Colin asked. Maybe he was the one that spoke just now.

"This has been a most trying day for me, gentlemen. You'll forgive me if I'm out of sorts." She smoothed the skirt of her green traveling dress. Their talk had her so upset she hadn't remembered to open her parasol against the sun. She did so now, almost stabbing Harrison in the eye. "Oh, I beg your pardon!" she said.

"Quite so," he said brightly, recovering from where he'd ducked. "Can happen to anyone." They helped her climb onto the wagon seat, then loaded her trunk and satchel in the back. He hopped into the wagon bed with her luggage.

Colin sat beside her to drive. "Right, then." He gave the horses a slap with the lines. "We're off!"

The wagon lurched forward and Pleasant grabbed at the seat to keep her balance. "How far out of town is your ranch?"

"Just a few miles," Colin said. "We'll be there in no time. You can have another cup of tea while you wait for your bath water to heat."

"You're sure it's no trouble for your wives?"

"None at all," Harrison said from behind them. "Besides, we're quite adept at handling mail-order brides around here. Heaven knows we've had enough of them."

"You have?" she said in shock and turned on the seat to face him. "How many mail-order brides?"

"We've hosted over a half-dozen at the ranch," he told her with a grin. "Though we were related to most of them, they were still mail-order brides. But we've had others come through over the years."

"Needless to say, dear lady," Colin said. "You're not the first, nor are you likely to be the last. And don't worry—Eli knows what he's doing, as does his brother."

"His brother?"

"Yes—Sheriff Tom Turner, Eli's older brother."

"Oh," she said. "Do they have other relations in town?"

"Yes, their sister Emeline. We'll let Eli fill you in on all that."

"We'll have enough trouble filling you in on our family, should you care to ask about it," Harrison said from behind them.

She didn't bother turning around this time. "I take it your family is a large one?"

"Oh yes!" they said in unison.

Still in shock from everything else that had happened that day, Pleasant forbore from asking any more questions. What had she allowed herself to get into?

Chapter Four

The Triple-C Ranch was not what Pleasant expected. It was something between a plantation and a compound, with two large two-story ranch houses, a smaller one, a huge barn and several small outbuildings. There was also a small cabin on a hill about fifty yards away and what she thought might be a bunkhouse near the barn. Just how big was this place? The Cooke family must do quite well indeed. "Whatever do you raise here?"

"Cattle, mostly," Harrison said. "Though we've branched out into horses of late."

"But our stock and trade, Miss Comfort, are cattle," Colin informed her. "The horses we raise for ourselves, not to sell. The Jones brothers own the main horse-breeding ranch around here, and I doubt we could compete with them."

"The Jones brothers?"

"Seth and Ryder. Their ranch is several miles on the other side of Clear Creek. They raise some of the finest horses in the state there."

"Some of the finest in the *Northwest*," Harrison corrected.

"I believe so," Colin said. "If you're in the market for a fine horse, they're the ones to see."

Pleasant nodded slowly as Colin brought the wagon to a stop in front of what she assumed was the main ranch house. The ranch and its grounds were pristine and well-kept, and a pang of jealousy struck as she remembered her beloved Comfort Fields with its park-like grounds. Would she ever see it again?

According to Aunt Phidelia, no, she wouldn't. Her running away had seen to that, and the thought pummeled her with guilt. Her father may have been about ready to lose everything; her departure had assured it. Her family had probably already disowned her—and at this point, she couldn't say that she blamed them. There would be no going back...

"Colin! Harrison!" a woman called from the front porch. "Where have you been?"

Pleasant pulled herself from her thoughts. The woman wore a simple blue calico dress and apron. Her brown hair was braided and piled on top of her head, but stray wisps floated on the breeze around her face. And she had the most beautiful blue eyes. Was she a servant?

"There you are, wife!" Harrison called as he hopped down, then lifted Pleasant's trunk out of the back of the wagon. "We have a houseguest."

Okay, decidedly not a servant. Pleasant glanced around the grounds a second time. Did these people *have* servants?

"I can see that," the woman said. "Don't tell me... is this Eli's mail-order bride?" She had a Southern accent, but quite different from Pleasant's—Texas, maybe?

"One and the same." Colin carried Pleasant's satchel

onto the front porch and handed it to the woman. "Sadie, meet Miss Comfort."

The woman arched an eyebrow at her. "How do you do?"

"Very well, thank you," Pleasant said from her perch on the wagon seat. "And you?"

"I'm just dandy." The woman looked her up and down. "Colin, help Miss Comfort down so she can come inside. She's probably tired after such a long journey." She turned to her husband. "Harrison, where's Eli?"

"Remember that outlaw gambling house Tom told us about the other day?"

"Oh no," she said in alarm. "Did they go after them?"

"Yes, dear wife, and I suspect they'll be hauling them in later this evening. We happened upon Eli as he was riding out of town after them. He told us to take care of Miss Comfort here until he returned," he said as he watched Colin helped Pleasant out of the wagon.

Pleasant went to stand before Sadie, but before she could say anything the woman grabbed her hand and pulled her into the house. "You poor thing! Come into the kitchen and we'll fix you right up! Harrison, put her things in the girls' room."

"You heard the woman," Harrison told his brother. "To the girls' room!" He snatched up the satchel and headed up the flight of stairs next to them in the foyer.

Colin shook his head. "I should've seen that coming and grabbed the satchel myself." He hefted Pleasant's trunk onto his shoulder and headed for the staircase.

"You'll have to be quicker next time," Sadie said with a laugh. She then led Pleasant down the hall and into a huge kitchen.

"Oh my, this is a large room," Pleasant remarked. "And Harri—Col—one of the gentlemen said you have a large family. I hope I'll be able to keep track of them all…eventually."

"It's okay if it takes a while. I'm sure everyone will introduce themselves properly when you meet them. I gather Harrison and Colin did so in town?"

"Yes, they did. I also had the, er…pleasure of meeting a Mr. and Mrs. Dunnigan."

Sadie's eyes widened, and she chuckled deep in her throat. "Well, I can't think of two better people to meet your first day in town—if only to get it over with. Irene Dunnigan is…well, we do have a few odd characters in town, but she's the only one that's in any way dangerous."

"I see!" Though she wasn't sure she did.

"In fact, the Dunnigans are Colin's in-laws of sorts. He's married to their niece Belle. She and Colin live in the house next door. They used to live in this one with Harrison and me, but we outgrew this one years ago. Too many children."

"How many families live on this ranch?"

"Well, Harrison and our four children live here. Colin and Belle and their five live next door. The smaller house belongs to our foreman Logan Kincaid and his family, and the cabin is occupied by Jefferson Cooke and his wife Edith. Jefferson is Colin and Harrison's stepfather. And of course, the ranch hands sleep in the bunkhouse."

Pleasant would feel more at home here than she thought. "I declare, you do have a large operation here." She glanced around the huge kitchen. "Where's your cook?"

Sadie laughed. "You're looking at her."

Pleasant's jaw dropped. "You mean you actually cook for that many people?"

"No—I cook for a lot more than that when you throw in the ranch hands. But I have myself and four other women to help me. Well, three and Belle's daughter, but she's not quite a woman yet—she's only fourteen."

Speaking of fourteen, Pleasant's eyes fixed on the huge kitchen table. It was long enough to seat at least that many. "How many people live in this house?"

"Just the six of us, but this was the original ranch house, so everyone gathers here. I guess it's what we're all used to. More often than not, Colin and his family and Jefferson and Edith eat supper here. Would you like a cup of tea or coffee?"

"Tea would be lovely, thank you." Pleasant then remembered something. "I hope it's not too much trouble, but the men spoke of…"

"I'll heat the water for a bath while you have your tea. Are you hungry?"

Pleasant stared at her, her mouth half-open. "You knew what I was going to say?"

Sadie smiled. "Oh, we've taken care of enough mail-order brides over the years to know the routine. You're probably tired, hungry and desperate for a hot bath, am I right?"

"That about sums it up."

"Then let's take care of you, shall we? By the time you meet your future groom, you'll feel like a new woman."

Pleasant sighed wearily. "I certainly hope so, Mrs. Cooke. At this point, I'd like to be." If she was, maybe she could forget what she'd done to her family.

* * *

"Dagnabit!" Sheriff Tom Turner huffed as he crouched next to his brother behind an outcropping of rock. He was breathing hard, as was Eli.

"They got us pinned, Tom," Eli said. "Where are the others?"

"I think Anson and Bran are over behind those trees." The group from Clear Creek had chased the outlaws to the tree line that bordered the prairie to the north of town. It was a good place to get ambushed because of the many outcroppings of rocks and boulders.

A shot rang out before Eli could reply, ricocheting off one of the rocks above their heads. "Consarnit! That was close!"

"Too close," Tom agreed. "Sorry ya hafta be out here on yer weddin' day."

"This ain't my weddin' day, brother. I plan on courtin' her first." Another shot, another ricocheting bullet. Both men glanced quickly around. "That is, if'n I get the chance."

"Ya will. My guess is Anson and Bran are tryin' to circle around behind 'em. We best keep them busy so they can do that."

"What's our brother-in-law doin' helpin' us anyway?" Eli asked.

"He was ridin' into town as I was ridin' out. Ya must've still been talkin' to the Cooke brothers. He's a good shot, and the more the better, I figger. Besides, Henry's gettin' too old for this sort of thing. Ya know how bad his eyesight is nowadays."

"I know. Just so long as we don't make our sister a widow today, I'm fine with it. Bad enough we're out here."

"Yeah, but it is our job," Tom countered.

Eli peered around the rock and took aim. "True, but sometimes I think we don't get paid enough for this. Heck, Anson don't get paid at all." He fired, the sound of the gunshot immediately followed by the scream of a man. "Bullseye. Got him right in the butt. That'll teach him to turn tail and run."

Tom shook his head before he also took aim. "Li'l brother, ya like what ya do. In fact, I'd go so far as to say ya'd do it whether ya got paid or not." He fired. Another scream rent the air.

"Doc Drake's sure gonna be busy later," Eli commented with a smile.

Tom grinned. "He sure enough is. And nobody's fault but theirs." He glanced off to one side and nodded. "There go Anson and Bran. Let's give 'em some cover, shall we?"

"Yessir." Eli gave his gun a twirl. The brothers stood and opened fire. Eli had counted at least eight outlaws, but with two of them wounded the odds were improved. He and Tom had wanted to round them up and get them locked away before the noon stage got in. But he'd had a feeling that morning that it might take longer than expected, so he'd asked the Cooke brothers to meet his future bride if he didn't get back to town in time.

Sure enough, it was after three o'clock now and he was worried they might not get it wrapped up before sundown. It was a good thing Anson White had tagged along—the man was a good shot, better than Henry, and maybe better than Eli and Bran. But no one was better than Tom, and between the four of them, they had the advantage.

More gunshots were heard, but they were coming from Anson and Bran, who'd managed to get behind the varmints and flush them into the open. Two of them limped out—make that three—with their hands in the air and no guns in sight. "Don't shoot!" one of them cried. "We're unarmed!"

"What about yer friends?" Tom yelled. Neither he nor Eli were fool enough to come out in the open for what might be a decoy.

More men began to emerge from behind trees and rocks, and Eli did a headcount. "That's thirteen out of fifteen. Where are the other two?"

"The other three," Tom corrected. "I don't see Snake, Frog, or their leader, Lizard."

"Lizard, gizzard, buzzard," Eli grumbled with a roll of his eyes. "Where do these outlaws get such silly names?"

"Everyone wants to be famous, li'l brother," Tom said. "My guess is they sacrificed these fellas so they can make a run for it."

"Poor saps." Eli stepped out from behind their cover and aimed his gun at the bedraggled group of men as they approached. "Toss yer guns, gents, or we'll shoot 'em outta yer hands." The few pistols remaining quickly dropped to the ground.

Anson and Deputy Bran O'Hare emerged from the trees, their guns also trained on the outlaws. "I sure hope I brought enough rope," Tom commented as he noted their catch.

"I've got extra in my saddlebag—don't worry," said Eli.

They quickly rounded the outlaws up, handcuffed those they could and bound the others' hands behind their backs. Eli ordered them into a line and used the remaining rope to string the outlaws together to lead them back to town on foot. One of them, younger than the rest, gave him a pleading look. "Please, Deputy, mah horse is back thar."

"Yers and everyone else's, I 'spect," Eli said, tying the rope around the man's waist, placing him last in line.

"Ya don't unnerstand. Mitzi, she's gonna foal. Ah shouldn't even be ridin' 'er."

Eli looked at him in shock. "Yer darn tootin' ya shouldn't. What idjit rides a horse about to foal?!"

The youth hung his head. "She ain't *that* close, but close 'nough. She's a good horse, 'n the sire's a might fine piece o' horseflesh too. If'n Ah'm goin' to jail for the rest o' mah life or…or gonna hang, I wanna make sure she's taken care of."

Eli studied him a moment. "How old are ya?"

He straightened. "Fourteen."

"Fourteen! What got ya tied up with these fellas, if'n ya don't mind my askin'?"

"See the one up at the front o' the line? That's mah brother Teddy. He tole me to come along. He knew Ah didn't have no other horse to ride."

"Told ya to come along and be an outlaw?" Eli asked in shock. "Do yer folks know where ya are? Where do ya live?"

The young man's cheeks flamed red under the dirt and grime on his face. "Oregon City."

"And ya just decided to up and join this bunch?" Eli asked.

"Er, yessir, I s'pose." He looked away again.

"How long ya been running with these men?"

"A little over two months."

Eli thought a moment as he studied the youth. He was no longer a boy, but not quite a man. He remembered what he was like at that age. His older brother either had a huge influence on him, or threatened him to get him to join up. "What's yer horse's name again?"

"Mitzi. She's the gray mare with the black mane 'n tail. Real purty. Promise me ya'll find a good home for 'er?"

Eli finished tying the knot and patted the kid on the back. "I promise."

"Thank ya, Deputy," he said with a genuine smile of relief. "Thanks a lot."

"Don't mention it. What's yer name?"

"Ninian, sir. Ninian Rush."

"Ninian? That's a different sorta name."

"Yeah. Teddy calls me Ninny for short."

"Not real brotherly of him, is it?"

"No, guess not," the youth agreed. "My ma usta call me Nan."

"Used to?"

Ninian met his gaze. "She died 'bout three months back. Our pa's gone too."

"So your brother Teddy came along, gathered ya up and thought he'd teach ya his business?"

"That's 'bout the size o' it, Deputy."

Eli sighed. Poor kid. "Well, Nan is better than Ninny, I guess." He sighed once more as he studied the boy again. "I'll take good care of Mitzi for ya, Ninian. And the foal too."

"Can I…if'n I'm able, come get 'er?"

Eli saw the love the boy had for his horse. "Sure. Soon as yer able."

Ninian nodded before he straightened and faced forward, a look of firm resolve now on his face. The youth was ready to face whatever was next. Eli hoped the judge would go easy on him. He'd have to make sure Ninian told the judge everything he'd just told him.

Tom gave a loud whistle to signal they were about to leave. Eli mounted his horse and rode over to his brother. "I've got somethin' to pick up and take back to town. I'll catch up to ya."

"What is it?" Tom asked.

"The boy's horse. Told him I'd keep it for a while."

"Boy?" Tom turned in his saddle to face him. "How old?"

"Says he's fourteen."

Tom shook his head. "Land sakes, they get younger and younger. All right, go round up their horses and take them over to Chase at the livery."

Eli nodded, spun his horse around and headed for the trees. He wondered what caused the boy to join his brother in an outlaw gang, other than the loss of his parents. Whatever it was, he hoped it didn't ruin his life for good. He pushed the thought aside—the sooner he and the others got this band of ne'er-do-wells locked up, the sooner he could meet his mail-order bride. He just hoped he didn't discover that the outlaws were better company.

"You do all your own laundry?" Pleasant asked, her voice a little shaky. She needed to get a hold of herself.

"Oh, I know it sounds like a lot of work." Sadie crossed the kitchen and grabbed an iron kettle off the stove. "But it's not if you have enough help. My daughter Honoria has become quite an accomplished cook."

Pleasant studied the pretty girl sitting across the kitchen table from her, peeling potatoes. Honoria Cooke looked to be the same age as Pleasant, with her mother's long, thick, sable brown hair and her father's dark eyes. She was beautiful and would have no problem fetching a husband, that was for sure. "So are you proficient at sewing too?" she asked the girl.

"I'm not, but I'm better than my sister."

"Your sister is barely ten years old," Sadie reminded her.

Honoria smirked at her mother. "You weren't supposed to say that, Mama."

Pleasant smiled. "I wish I had a little sister to compare my skills to. Maybe I'd feel better about them."

"I get the impression you haven't sewn much." Sadie said.

"Not unless you count embroidery—that's the extent of my experience. I can't tell you how much it pains me to admit that."

"My sister can't admit she's not as good a seamstress as I am," Honoria volunteered. "She's stubborn that way."

"I'm afraid I have no excuse like your sister—I'm certainly not ten." Pleasant sighed. "No, I'm just inexperienced. Where I came from there was no need to learn."

"Where is that?" Honoria asked.

Pleasant hesitated. Should she tell them? What if her brothers came looking for her? But if they did, they wouldn't be looking for a woman from Savannah per se, but a dark-haired Southern girl named Pleasant Comfort. Never mind her accent or anything else—the name was enough. "Savannah, Georgia," she finally said.

"Savannah?" Sadie exclaimed with a smile. "Why, that's the name of our youngest!"

Pleasant glanced between the two smiling women. "It is? Well, I feel flattered in a way."

"I've always loved that name," Sadie said. "She's playing with her brothers at Colin and Belle's place. They'll be home soon."

"I'd love to meet her. She's the ten-year-old, I take it?"

"Yes, she is. She's inquisitive, just as stubborn as her sister says, and very much a tomboy too. But with two older brothers and all those male cousins…"

Pleasant nodded. Maybe if her family had more cousins, they wouldn't be in such dire straits. Perhaps some uncles could have helped her father before he got himself into trouble. But alas, there were no such. Her father was an only child—Aunt Phidelia was his only living relative besides his children.

Pleasant's eyes darted around the homey kitchen and she felt a pinch of envy. She hoped she'd have a house such as Sadie's one day. Then perhaps, surrounded by the nice people of Clear Creek and with a loving husband, she could be happy.

Chapter Five

By the time supper rolled around, Pleasant had bathed, washed her hair and even gotten a brief rest in. Honoria helped her dress and marveled at her gown. "It's so beautiful!"

"Thank you. It was a gift from my father for my eighteenth birthday."

"When was that?"

"February. When's yours?"

"I'll be eighteen in June."

Pleasant smiled. "Do you have a beau?"

Something in Honoria's eyes flashed, but Pleasant wasn't sure why. Was she angry at the question? "No. There aren't many gentlemen around here to choose from. The only one closest to my age is…" She glanced at the ceiling with a small groan. "Eli Turner."

"Eli? My Eli?" Good heavens, was there something wrong with the man? Honoria Cooke was a beauty to behold, just like her mother. What man wouldn't want to marry her?

"Yes, but we would never suit."

"Why ever not?" she asked, trying not to sound worried.

Honoria shrugged. "We don't see eye to eye on things."

"What do you mean? Is the man not agreeable?"

"Oh no, don't get me wrong. I like Eli, very much. But…well, the best way to put it is that I'm rather opinionated. About pretty much everything."

Pleasant stared at her a moment, then laughed. "You sound like one of my brothers."

"Pray I never meet him. We'd probably kill each other."

Pleasant's smile faded. "I see no reason to worry. I doubt you'd ever have the pleasure."

"Your family doesn't plan on visiting you at some point?"

"No, I…don't see that happening. I shall have to go to them." Not that that was likely either…

"Oh, that's too bad. It's always fun to meet new people around here. Speaking of which, we'd better get downstairs. Mama and Auntie Belle will want to introduce you to the family if you're having supper with us."

"Yes, of course." She glanced at her blue gown. "I'm not overdressed?"

Honoria noted her simple yellow calico. "No, I'm underdressed—as will be the rest of my family. Sorry about that."

Pleasant laughed again. She was beginning to like Honoria and hoped they'd become good friends. "I'll forgive you and your family."

"Thank you, Miss Comfort."

"Please, call me Pleasant."

Honoria cocked her head to one side and smiled. "That's a fitting name."

Pleasant blushed and smiled. "Thank you for that."

"Shall we?" Honoria swept a hand toward the bedroom door.

Pleasant preceded her and they went downstairs where the families were gathering for supper. And what a gathering it was! "There are so many!"

"This is nothing," Honoria remarked. "You should see when the cousins are here."

"I can only imagine." Pleasant noted all the children happily chatting away or playing, not to mention the adults, who at this point were staring at her.

"Here we are!" Honoria announced.

Sadie made her way through the crowd. "Everyone come into the parlor and meet our guest!" she yelled.

No sooner had she said it than children came from every room and ran for the parlor, several running into Pleasant in the process. She almost fell over, but Honoria caught her just in time. "My word!"

"I'm sorry about that. The little ones are always excited when we have a guest."

"You won't have one if they trample me," Pleasant replied, trying to keep her temper in check. She kept having to remind herself she was no longer in Savannah. This was the Wild West—which obviously included wild children.

"That's it, gather 'round!" Sadie called as Honoria guided Pleasant into the center of the room.

"There now, I think we're all here," someone said. Pleasant recognized the voice—it was Harrison, Sadie's husband. She hadn't even noticed him in the crowd.

"All right everyone, line up as best you can and we'll proceed with the introductions," Sadie said loudly.

Children scrambled to comply. They ranged from

what Pleasant guessed to be about nine or ten up to sixteen or seventeen. "Who's the oldest?"

"I am," Honoria said with a hint of pride.

"Are we ready?" Sadie asked then turned to Pleasant. "Now, I know you're not going to remember them all after introductions. But they so wanted to make your acquaintance."

Pleasant smiled and nodded. "There are...so many. Surely they're not all yours. That is, you and your sister-in-law's."

"Oh heavens, no," a woman said from behind her. "Some of these belong to Logan, our foreman."

Pleasant turned to face a pretty woman with dark blonde hair. "How do you do?"

"Very well. I'm Belle Cooke." She grabbed one of Pleasant's hands and gave it a healthy shake, then glanced at everyone gathered and back again. "You'd best brace yourself."

Pleasant's eyebrows rose in worry. "So it seems."

Sadie put her hands on her hips. "Of course you already know Honoria." She stepped to the line of children and pointed to a handsome dark-haired boy with hazel eyes. "This is Maxwell, and next to him is Clinton and standing behind him is Savannah." The boys looked very much alike, only one was shorter than the other. Savannah, a blonde with the same eyes as her brothers, peeked around Clinton and smiled at her.

Pleasant gave the children a small curtsy. "How do you do?"

Savannah giggled as her brothers blushed and fidgeted.

"They're a little shy at first," Harrison said.

"Colin you know, and now Belle," Sadie continued.

"And these are their children, Jefferson, Adele, Thackary, Sam and, last but not least, Parthena."

Pleasant could only stare. All the Cooke children were comely, no wonder considering their parents. "How old are they?" she asked.

"Jefferson, our oldest, will be sixteen in November," Colin said. "Little Theena just turned nine."

"Theena—what a lovely nickname," said Pleasant.

"We think so," Colin said with pride. "And may I introduce Harrison's and my stepfather Jefferson and his wife Edith." An older man and his wife stepped forward. They looked to be somewhere in their sixties, the same as the Dunnigans.

"Hello," she greeted.

"We don't stand on no fancy ceremony here!" the man barked then grabbed her in a hug.

Pleasant grunted in response. "Oh! Well, so nice… to meet…you."

"Let go of her, Jefferson, before she expires for lack of breath!" his wife said. But as soon as he let her go, Edith grabbed her in the same manner.

This naturally resulted in the same grunt. "Oh my, how friendly…you all are."

Edith let go and gave her hand a vigorous shake. "Nice to have ya here!"

Pleasant took a step back so she could catch her breath. She unconsciously smoothed the skirt of her dress as she did and sucked in a lungful of air.

"And this is Logan Kincaid our foreman and his wife Susara," Sadie went on.

Good grief! There's more? Pleasant thought as she smiled at the dark-haired man and his pretty blonde wife.

"Hello," she managed then braced herself. She wasn't sure she could survive any more vigorous hugging.

Thankfully, they shook her hand instead. "Welcome to Clear Creek," Susara said.

Pleasant nodded and smiled.

Sadie then pointed to the children behind them. There were so many people in the parlor they were spilling out into the foyer. "And here we have Owen, Martin, Ferris and... Eli!"

Pleasant jumped. "Eli?" she whispered and tried to see past the Kincaids.

"Eli! What are you doing here?" Sadie asked as she waded through the children toward the front door.

A man stood in the foyer, surrounded by several children of varying ages. His dark eyes locked with Pleasant's blue ones. His breath caught and for a moment he looked as if he couldn't speak. "I..." He swallowed hard. "Well, ain't it obvious? I'm here to fetch my bride."

Everyone standing between Eli and his bride parted. It was all Eli could do to talk. She was so lovely she literally took his breath away. His stomach flipped itself into a frenzy and his hands began to sweat. *That vision in the blue gown...is mine?* he thought to himself. He could scarcely believe it—yet there she was, the only one in the room he didn't know. But he would—oh yes indeed, he would.

That is, if he could get his feet to move. He gulped back his initial shock and slowly made his way toward her. The entire house had gone quiet as everyone, even the younger children, watched him approach. When he finally reached her his mouth slowly fell open as he gawked, his hat in his hands.

Honoria stepped over to him and elbowed him in the ribs.

Eli jumped. "Howdy!" he squawked. "I'm… I'm Eli Turner, ma'am."

Her eyes were as wide as his. He hoped she wasn't as shocked at his appearance as he was at hers. If she was, was it a good shock or bad? He knew he wasn't as handsome as the Cooke men or others in town, but he wasn't hideous either. He was just Eli, like his brother was just Tom, or their sister was just Emeline. Nothing special about any of them, as far as he was concerned.

"How do you do?" the vision standing before him said.

Her smooth Southern accent took his breath away all over again, and he smiled. "Well, I'll be. Say somethin' else."

She looked nervously at the others. "Excuse me?"

Eli's smiled broadened. "Beggin' your pardon, ma'am, but ya got the purtiest accent I ever did hear."

"Did you hear that, brother?" Colin called to Harrison across the room. "Our accents have become commonplace."

"I dare say, it was bound to happen," Harrison replied in amusement.

Eli's bride glanced around again. "We were in the middle of introductions, Mr. Turner. It seems you arrived just in time to…join in."

Was she joking? But there were a lot of folks crowded into the one room—at least twenty if his guess was right…

"Okay, enough!" Sadie called out. "Children, you know where to go!"

The children scrambled for the kitchen, almost

knocking Eli over. He stood his ground in order to shield the woman standing before him—he didn't want to see her get trampled. But he needn't have worried—she stood, feet apart, bracing herself against the torrent making its way out of the parlor. Their eyes met and locked as children bumped past them.

Once they cleared the room, Eli smiled at her. "Howdy…um, I'm yer intended, Eli Turner. Sorry I wasn't in town earlier today to meet the stage."

She smiled tentatively in return. He almost swooned on the spot—what a pretty mouth she had! "I understand you were preoccupied."

He nodded grimly. "Sure was."

Her eyes roamed over him. "I trust the situation with the outlaws is well in hand?"

He suddenly straightened. "Oh yes, ma'am. We done got them varmints locked up and wired for the judge to come."

"Judge? You mean you haven't one in this town?"

"Not yet, no—just a circuit judge that comes from Oregon City. We sent a message so he'll come 'round."

She slowly nodded as she studied him, looking as if she was trying to take in as much of him as she could before they left the room. Which everyone else had—only Sadie and Harrison remained in the parlor with them now.

"Would you like to join us for supper, Deputy?" Sadie asked. "I'll set another plate."

"Thanks, Sadie," he said, never taking his eyes off of…good grief, what was her name again? Comfortable? No, that couldn't be right. It would come to him. Dag, maybe he should've taken a nap before coming over—he didn't feel very sharp. "Much obliged," he finished.

"I'll seat you across from Miss Comfort." Sadie left the parlor.

Comfort! How could he forget a name like that?

Harrison cleared his throat. "Ahem…" Eli and Miss Comfort both slowly turned to him, and he couldn't help grinning. "Why don't you escort your future bride into the dining room, Eli?"

"Oh! Oh yeah." He offered her his arm. Her eyes flicked between his arm and his face a few times before she took it, and he almost sighed in relief. He took a deep breath and escorted Miss Comfort into supper.

Suppertime at the Triple-C, Sadie explained while setting an extra place for Eli, involved both the kitchen and dining room. The children, Jefferson and Edith took the kitchen table, while the other adults used the dining room. This arrangement worked especially well when Logan, Susara and their brood joined them. The kitchen table sat fourteen and the dining table twelve, but Eli was still surprised there were empty seats left.

"Don't seem the same 'round here without Duncan," he commented as he pulled out a chair for Miss Comfort.

She sat, an astonished look on her face. "There's more of them?!"

Colin and Harrison laughed. "Yes, our older brother Duncan and his wife," Harrison volunteered. "They reside in England now."

"For a time we had quite the houseful, even before the children started coming," Sadie added.

Eli smiled as he sat. "Sure is a nice place, the Triple-C. Always do enjoy comin' out here, never mind who's here."

Miss Comfort looked around the table, resplendent

with chintz place settings and steaming hot food. Sadie must have put out her best china for the occasion. "How nice. Everything looks wonderful."

"We aren't completely uncivilized out here, Miss Comfort," Belle said jokingly. "Though I'm sure Clear Creek is still a far cry from Savannah."

"Indeed it is," she said. "Tell me, where are you from? I detect a slight accent."

"Boston, originally, but I've lived here for nearly twenty years."

"So long?"

Eli stared at her. "Well, I've lived here all my life. My sister even longer."

She looked up from admiring her place setting. "I would imagine so, Mr. Turner. Especially if she's an older sister."

Eli wanted to groan. Could he have made himself sound dumber? Maybe he'd better shut up while he was ahead.

Thankfully, Colin bowed his head to give the blessing. When he was done, they began to eat. "Mmm…my compliments, Mrs. Cooke. This pot roast is outstanding," Miss Comfort said.

"It's Mrs. Dunnigan's recipe," Harrison said. "Quite a few women in town use it."

"Mrs. Dunnigan? From the mercantile?"

"Yes, my aunt," Belle put in.

"Oh yes—your husband informed me earlier." Miss Comfort glanced around the table. "Do all your relatives live in Clear Creek?"

"Mine don't," said Mr. Kincaid. "I got me an older brother back in Texas."

"Have you seen him since you've lived here?" Miss Comfort asked.

"'Fraid not."

She paled and stopped eating, a horrified look on her face. "And…how long have you lived here, Mr. Kincaid?" she asked weakly.

"Let's see, I started working for the Cookes back in… '58, '59? Consarnit, I can't remember. It was before the war…"

"It was '58," Susara told him.

Miss Comfort set her fork down. "So you haven't seen your family since then?"

"Nope."

She looked away, her eyes closed, as if to shut them against great pain.

"Are you all right, Miss Comfort?" It was the first time Eli had used her name, and he realized that he didn't even know what her first name was. She'd signed her letter P.A. Comfort, and P could stand for just about anything…

She looked at him, her eyes slightly misted. "Quite all right, Mr. Turner. Thank you for asking."

He nodded, not sure of what he could do for her. She wasn't all right, he could tell. Maybe she was homesick, and the thought of going years without seeing her family pained her greatly. He hoped that as her husband, he'd be able to ease that pain—and silently vowed to do whatever he could to see it done.

Chapter Six

After supper the children went outside to play hide-and-seek in the barnyard. "Is it difficult having so many children living on one ranch?" Miss Comfort asked Belle.

"Not at all. There are only twelve altogether."

"Yes, of course, but what about school?"

"I take them with me," Susara said. "I'm the town schoolteacher."

Miss Comfort's eyes widened. "You are?" She quickly looked at Eli. "Were you Mr. Turner's teacher?"

Susara smiled and glanced between the two of them. "Indeed I was."

Pleasant watched him give a tiny shake of his head. She'd done her best not to be too obvious in her perusal of him during the meal, but it wasn't easy. He wasn't as polished as her brothers, but there was something incredibly attractive about him, more than just being handsome. He had…presence, as her mother would have said. There was an easygoing confidence in how he carried himself, the way he sat and conversed with everyone at the table.

But she was curious to know how well-educated he was. He certainly didn't speak like an educated man. "Mrs. Kincaid? Forgive me if I'm... I was wondering..."

Susara seemed to be amused by her half-question. "Eli was a good student, if that's what you were wondering," Susara said. "He had excellent penmanship."

Pleasant noticed him fidgeting, and wondered what the schoolmarm was leaving out. "Did he, now?"

"Yes, though there were some incidents..."

Eli gulped.

"...such as the time he wrapped up a box of beetles and gave them to me for Christmas."

A hand flew to Pleasant's mouth to stifle a giggle. "He did?"

"Oh yes," Susara said, smiling at Mr. Turner. "He was also very good at tying knots. He once tied his sister to a tree behind the schoolhouse. It took me a while to discover her."

Mr. Turner groaned.

"Discover her?" Pleasant asked, a little shocked. "Didn't she call for help?"

"Emeline? Heavens no, she was far too proud a child for that. Actually, she was trying to chew through the ropes when I found her."

Mr. Turner began to laugh nervously. "Oh my—I'd plumb forgot 'bout that!"

Pleasant looked at him, aghast. "I'm sure your sister hasn't."

"I'm sure she hain't. But I did a lot worse to her growin' up—and she to me. After all, she is my *big* sister."

Pleasant wanted to ask what sort of things, but Belle and Sadie were bringing in dessert along with Jefferson and Edith. They had coffee and pie while the children devoured two plates of cookies. "Which child is the youngest?"

"Theena," Sadie said. "Though it's close. There are three nine year-olds here on the ranch—she just happens to trail the others by a couple of months."

"And our oldest is seventeen," Harrison said. "Eighteen, once Honoria has her birthday in June."

Pleasant nodded. Huge families like this weren't uncommon in the South, nor living so close together. But even there, the Cookes would be larger than most. "Am I to understand that you take a wagon full of children to town with you every day for school?" she asked Susara.

"Yes, that's right." Susara took a sip of her coffee. "It wasn't as easy when they were younger, but we managed. Winters are the worst."

"Winters?" Pleasant said, her voice barely audible. Good heavens, how could she forget about winters? This far north, that meant cold—and she hated the cold.

"They ain't as bad as all that," Mr. Turner told her, his voice gentle. "Not if yer prepared for 'em."

"I wouldn't be too worried, Missy," Jefferson said. "You'll be snug and warm out at Eli's place. It's so tiny, it's easy to heat."

Her eyes swiveled to him. "Tiny?"

"Sure—one room don't need much in the way of heatin'."

One room? Did she hear him right?

"'Course, I plan on addin' onto it," Mr. Turner said quickly. "'Specially once we start havin' younguns."

Pleasant tensely looked around the beauty of the dining room. This was a normal environment for her. But the Triple-C was obviously quite prosperous. Her future husband was a deputy, a simple lawman—how much did he make? Only enough for a one-room cabin, apparently. She slumped in her chair, feeling a little faint.

"Hey now—ya sure yer okay?" Mr. Turner said. "Ya ain't sick, are ya?"

"Oh no, I'm fine." She quickly straightened up.

"That's a relief. I'd hate to hafta pay a visit to Doc Drake with ya. He's awful busy tonight patchin' up the outlaws we shot."

Pleasant's eyebrows headed for the ceiling. "Shot?! You shot someone today?" she squeaked.

"Well, yeah. I ain't gonna go into the particulars, ya bein' a lady and all, but they shot at us first, so we shot back. I got three of 'em myself."

Pleasant's eyes rolled back as her body dropped away into oblivion. If only she could stay there awhile.

"I didn't say shot dead!" Eli carried his future bride into the parlor and gently laid her on a red-tufted sofa. "Dang, I never saw a woman faint before." He looked at Colin and Harrison. "Are they like this for long?"

The brothers looked at one another. "I suppose it depends on how great the shock was," Colin said.

"She's still out," Harrison said. "You must have given her a big one, Eli."

"What?! Me?" Eli cast a worried glance at Miss Comfort. "What do I do?"

"You do nothing," Sadie said, kneeling on the floor next to the sofa. She picked up one of Miss Comfort's hands and began to pat it as Belle fanned her with a hankie.

Much to Eli's surprise, it worked. Her eyes began to flutter open, and he sighed in relief. It wouldn't do to have his future bride expire on him her first day in town. He felt so helpless when it came to things like this. A fainting woman, in his book, was best left to other females to deal with.

"What happened?" she asked as Sadie helped her up. "Did I faint?"

"You did," Belle said matter-of-factly. "Though I can't say I blame you." She raised an eyebrow at Eli, who cringed in return. Clearly women from the South weren't used to hearing about outlaws being shot. But he was a lawman—it was part of his job. He certainly hoped she toughened up quickly—he didn't know if he could tend to a fainting woman every day of the week…

"I think for now, Eli, you'd better keep those sorts of things to yourself," Sadie whispered. "At least until the two of you get to know each other better."

He nodded. Not a bad idea. "Colin, can I talk to ya for a minute?"

"Certainly." He glanced at Harrison.

Eli caught the exchange. "You too, Harrison, if'n ya don't mind."

"Not at all." The three men went out to the front porch. "I think I know what you're going to ask."

"I *know* what he's going to," Colin quipped. "You want to know if Miss Comfort can stay here so the two of you can court a bit."

Eli nodded. "Yep."

"But why?" asked Harrison. "She's beautiful, charming, spirited. A mite prone to shocks, but that should pass in time."

"What if I marry her and she cain't adjust to life out here?" Eli asked in all seriousness. "Ya saw what just happened."

Colin stood, hands on hips. "He has a point, brother.

We've not had anyone from the gentle South grace our town before."

"Oh yes we have," Harrison was quick to correct. "The Dunnigans are from… Alabama, was it?"

"The *gentle* South," Colin emphasized. "The plantations and all that."

"Ah, I see what you mean. Well, there was Thaddeus Slade…"

"Egads," Colin retorted. "Granted, he wasn't the fainting sort…"

"Who?" Eli asked, confused.

"Thaddeus Slade was originally from New Orleans," Colin explained. "He came to work on the hotel when Mr. Van Cleet was first building it. A horrible lecher—Harrison's wife can explain in depth if you have the stomach for it."

Eli looked at the brothers in shock. "How come Tom never told me none of this? Did ya shoot him?"

The brothers laughed. "No," Harrison managed through his chuckles. "Sadie curbed his ardor by hitting him with a hot frying pan."

Eli cringed. Sadie had gumption and lots of it. "That explains a lot. But… I don't think Miss Comfort in there's of the same mind should somethin' like that happen."

"Then you'll just have to defend your lady fair," Colin said. "Simple."

"Not when I'm gone all day deputyin'. Ya cain't expect me to take her along."

"Of course not," Harrison said. "You do what we did with our wives."

Eli glanced between them. "What was that?"

"We taught them how to defend themselves," Colin

said with a shrug. "After all the things that have happened around here over the years, we weren't about to leave them defenseless while we were out working."

Eli nodded. Clear Creek had seen its fair share of unsavory characters over the years. Most everyone was able to take on a little trouble, more if they banded together. He'd been so used to it that he figured everyone was of a like mind. But maybe folks from the South were different—or was it just his bride-to-be? "So what do ya suggest I do?"

"You teach her how," Colin said as if suggesting he teach her to bake cookies.

Eli ran a hand over his face. "What happens if she's terrible at it?" After all, did he really want to put a gun into his future wife's hands?

"Given enough time and effort, she'll get as good as our wives," Harrison said. "I don't see a problem."

Eli had a sudden vision of Miss Comfort shooting him in the foot. "I do!"

"Come now, man—pull yourself together!" Colin said with a laugh. "What could possibly happen?"

Eli glanced at the parlor window. "Plenty." Now all he had to do was pray he was wrong.

"But why do I have to stay here?" Pleasant asked Belle. "I thought Mr. Turner and I were to be married." Wasn't that what she came for?

"It will give the two of you time to get to know one another better," Belle told her as she helped her undress. "Besides, it's not like it's going to be forever."

It will be if he decides he doesn't like me, she thought. That alone had her tense. Everyone liked her at home.

As soon as she turned eighteen, she could've had her pick of gentlemen. All of them poor, but still… She sighed. No wonder her father had set his eyes on Rupert for her. He had money.

"I think he already likes you." Sadie hung up Pleasant's clothes in an armoire next to Honoria's. "But there are things you need to learn in order to stay safe out here."

"Safe? Oh dear—you mean against outlaws?"

"Against all sorts of things," Belle said and looked at Sadie. "Remember that time Ryder Jones was bitten by a rattlesnake, and Constance had to save him?"

"Oh yes. If she hadn't been able to ride well, he'd have been dead."

Pleasant was still a couple of sentences behind. "R-r-r-rattlesnake?!"

"Don't they have those where you come from?" Sadie asked.

"Yes, but…well, actually I don't know." She sat down hard on the bed. "I'm not particularly fond of snakes."

"Well, honestly, who is?" Belle replied. "Or what about the time Duncan was poisoned?"

"Yes—Mrs. MacDonald saved the day that time. Or when Maddie got shot?"

Pleasant jumped up off the bed. "Shot?!"

"Yes, after she jumped out of a speeding stagecoach," Belle added.

"Oh dear, oh dear, oh dear," Pleasant said, fanning herself with her hand. "What woman jumps out of a moving coach?"

"A desperate one," Sadie answered somberly. "She was taken against her will by some very bad men."

"After they shot her husband," Belle clarified.

Pleasant's knees went weak, and down she went.

When she came to this time it was on the floor, not a nice soft sofa. "Well, that tells us what we have to work with, doesn't it?" Sadie asked Belle as they hovered over her.

"Quite—it looks like we have our work cut out for us."

"Us? Oh no, this is Eli's problem, not ours. He's going to have to see to most of her learning."

"We can take care of some of it, though. And Honoria can help."

"She'll have to. We don't have the time to see to all of it."

Pleasant was confused. What on Earth were they talking about?

"All right—tomorrow's as good a day as any to start," Belle said. "The boys will want to help too."

"That might not be such a good idea," Sadie said.

Never mind what they were talking about—Pleasant knew she wanted no part of it.

"Hmm, perhaps you're right," Belle said. "They might play too rough."

"Then again, it might be good for them to learn more responsibility," said Sadie.

Belle sighed. "Well, if you say so—but if they get too rough, then no more. I'd hate to find poor Miss Comfort hanging by her ankles from a tree."

Pleasant's eyes popped open. "Tree?"

Both women looked at her. "Never mind," Sadie said, then pulled her to her feet. "Best you get into your bedclothes and call it a day."

"You'll need your rest, with your lessons starting tomorrow," Belle said.

"Lessons? What lessons?"

Sadie smiled. "How to be a Clear Creek woman. Now off to bed."

Chapter Seven

"Ohhhh," Pleasant groaned, "what a horrible night-mare." She opened her eyes, but didn't see her flowered bed canopy above her. "Merciful heavens, where am I?"

She sat upright and glanced around. The room was nothing fancy, the furniture well-made and sturdy but hardly intricate—nothing like those back home at Comfort Fields...

She fell back upon the bed and groaned again. "Oh, that's right." It was no dream—she had become a mail-order bride and was now out West...somewhere. She rolled over and buried her face in her pillow as everything came flooding back, including the two times she'd fainted. How was she ever to survive this barbaric country?

"Oh good, you're up," Belle declared as she came into the room. "I thought I heard you talking. Do you always talk to yourself in the morning? It's all right if you do—my Colin does."

Pleasant raised her head and looked at her. The least she could do was be civil to the woman. "No, I am not in the habit. Except when I've had a shock, perhaps."

Belle set a water pitcher on the dresser. "Have you?"

Pleasant managed a half-smile. "Oh yes. I even forgot where I was for a moment."

Belle tried not to laugh, and failed. "Then you have had a shock. No wonder you were talking to yourself."

Pleasant rolled over and stared at the ceiling. "I remember dreaming something about jumping out of a stagecoach and being shot at."

"That's probably from what Sadie and I talked about last night before you went to bed. Those things actually happened to Madeleine Van Zuyen."

"Who is Madeleine Van Zuyen, and why in Heaven's name would she jump from a moving stagecoach?"

"It's a long story," Belle said with a sigh. "One of these days we'll have to tell you about it, but right now it's almost time for breakfast. Best you get up and dressed."

Pleasant groaned and sat up again. "What time is it?"

"Just after six. We let you sleep in, as it's your first day here."

"Six o'clock? In the morning?" Pleasant shook her head. "Merciful heavens, one would think I'm a servant!"

"You're on a working cattle ranch now—we all serve here. Normally we get up at five, if not earlier."

Pleasant groaned and fell back onto her pillow again. "I don't think I've ever gotten up before nine," she muttered, throwing an arm over her eyes.

"Really?" Belle asked in bemused surprise.

Pleasant frowned. Obviously expecting sympathy at this point would be foolish. "I'm getting up. Please leave the room."

"Very well. I'll see you downstairs in the kitchen."

Pleasant waited for the click of the door latch before she removed her arm. She glanced around the room again as the reality of her situation hit hard and fast. She was in a strange place with a bunch of strange people, about to marry a stranger. "How utterly strange," she said with a laugh.

But there was nothing strange about running from a marriage to Rupert Jerney. She'd have been miserable with the man, and she knew it. She'd made this bed for herself out West, and now she would have to lie in it—even if there was a stranger in the bed also.

She got up, washed, dressed and fixed her hair as she'd learned to do so on the journey West. There were no servants to help her in her travels, nor were there any here at the Triple-C. And there certainly wouldn't be in Eli's—she shuddered—one-room cabin. Self-sufficiency was the order of the day here—and she'd have to adjust to it.

Downstairs she found Sadie, Belle and Honoria cooking breakfast. A group of children were already seated at the kitchen table. "Do you eat all your meals here?" Pleasant asked.

Belle turned from the stove. "Not always, but since you're here, we thought it might be fun."

"Fun? What's fun about a kitchen?"

"Cookies!" a little girl exclaimed happily. What was her name again—Tina? Theena? Parmeena? Oh heavens, she was never going to keep everyone's names sorted!

"I prefer cake," said the oldest boy. His name, she remembered—Jefferson. He'd obviously been named after Colin's stepfather.

Belle poured Pleasant a cup of coffee and handed

it to her. "We'll bake today, Jeff, with Miss Comfort's help. You do bake, don't you?"

"Back home…we had a cook," she explained reluctantly.

Jefferson glanced nervously between his mother and aunt. "Don't ask me to be a guinea pig later. I don't like burnt cake."

"You eat everything," his mother quipped. "Don't worry, we'll have Miss Comfort cooking up a storm in no time."

"Eli will appreciate that," Jefferson commented as he got up from the table and grabbed a few pieces of bacon off a plate. "I'm heading out, Mother."

"Fine." She handed him a small bag. "Take these biscuits to your father. They already have butter and jam on them."

The boy nodded, grabbed his hat off the back of the chair, put it on and left the kitchen through the back door.

"Is he going to school?" Pleasant asked.

"No, he's going out to help his father work today," Belle said. "Max and Clinton, Sadie's oldest, are already out there."

"They don't go to school?" Pleasant asked.

"Not today—it's Saturday. There's no school around here on Saturdays and Sundays." A couple of the other children giggled.

Pleasant shook her head—how had she lost track of the days? "Forgive my confusion." She glanced at the table, where five kids remained. "What will the other children do all day?"

Sadie set a plate of food on the table and motioned for Pleasant to sit. "Savannah and Parthena will help with the mending. Thackary and Samuel will be chopping wood." One of the boys made a disgruntled sound.

Pleasant met the eyes of the oldest girl—she looked to be about fourteen. "And the young lady?" It must have been the right thing to say—the girl smiled and blushed.

"Adele will be helping us with the baking," Belle informed her.

Pleasant sat as the smell of food wafted up from the plate in front of her, making her stomach growl. "What about the others?"

"Others?" Sadie asked.

Pleasant lay a napkin on her lap. "I… I was sure there were more children here last night…"

"Oh, you're referring to Logan and Susara's," Sadie said. "Logan probably has them out working the stock today."

Children, working with cattle?! "But they're so young!"

"Owen is fourteen, and Martin twelve," Belle said. "Ferris will be left behind—not because he's ten, but because he has other chores to do. Logan's boys like working with their father. Besides, it gets them out of chores like chopping wood."

"I don't mind chopping wood," said one of the boys at the table. But was it Thackary or Samuel?

"I do," the other one said. "It makes my hands hurt."

Pleasant smiled to herself. For the first time she noticed the Cooke children had a very light British accent. Come to think of it, Honoria did as well.

"Oh, toughen up, Sam," the first one—presumably Thackary—told him, punctuating his statement with a gentle elbow to Sam's bicep.

"I don't know how you keep track of all these children," Pleasant admitted. "I have six grown brothers and I can't keep track of them half the time."

Sadie laughed. "Perhaps that's because they're men, and they run off and do what they want. Around here, our children have to do what *we* want. There's the difference."

Samuel sighed unhappily, getting a dirty look from Thackary but no elbow.

Pleasant smiled in understanding. Would she ever have children? And if she did, how many? Could she handle having a child—or more to the point, could she handle doing it out here in the back of the beyond? Heavens, she wasn't even sure she could handle being married under these circumstances! And speaking of which… "Will Mr. Turner be coming out to the ranch today?"

"Of course," Sadie said. "We've invited him to supper."

Pleasant took a bite of her fried potatoes. Oh my—they were wonderful! "Have you known Mr. Turner a long time?"

"Since he was just a little shaver," Sadie said. "Belle and I watched him grow up. Tom too, though he was older when we came here."

"Tom was probably thirteen or fourteen when I came to Clear Creek," Belle agreed. "Emeline was maybe nine, which means Eli couldn't have been more than seven."

Pleasant smiled. At least she could ask them questions about her future husband. "Is he a…a good man?"

Sadie sat at the table with a cup of coffee. "If you're worried about marrying Eli Turner, don't. Eli is as good as they come, and always has been. What I'd worry about if I were you, is being a good wife to him. From what we learned about you last night…well, you have a lot to learn, and a lot of toughening up to do."

Pleasant's mouth fell open in shock. "I beg your pardon?"

Belle joined them at the table and sat, a plate of food in her hand. "It's nothing personal, Miss Comfort. Your fainting twice—that told us a lot."

"I never!" Pleasant said as her back went rigid.

"Now, now, don't get on your high horse about it," Sadie said. "We had to learn how to be wives to our men and ours are from England!"

"Yes, but the only difference between our husbands and the other men around here are their accents and a few mannerisms," Belle explained. "Other than that, they're just like anyone else in Clear Creek."

"What…what are you saying?" Pleasant asked nervously. She was beginning to wonder where this was going.

Sadie sighed. "Let's get down to brass tacks. How good a cook are you?"

"Um… I wouldn't really know. As I said, we had a cook…"

"How about cleaning? Sewing? Mending? Gathering firewood? Have you ever kept chickens? Milked a cow? Mopped floors?"

Sadie spoke gently, but every question was like an arrow in Pleasant's chest. "I see I'm not quite as prepared as I thought," she mumbled at her plate.

"Neither were we when we arrived here," Sadie assured her. "But those are all things you'll have to learn, just like we did."

"And that's not all," Belle said. "Out here, things

can get rough at times. There are storms, sometimes droughts, cattle rustlers, outlaws, sickness—and none of the luxuries of a big city like Boston or Savannah. Bluntly put, fainting is not an option here."

Pleasant needed a few seconds to absorb it all. "Oh dear. I apologize for being so quick to take offense. Why, I've never traveled more than ten miles out of Savannah—this is all very new to me."

"We understand," Sadie said. "We only want to help you. The sooner you learn how to get along out here, the better off you'll be. Eli's place is a couple of miles outside of town, and even though two of our cousins will be your neighbors, you'll still have to learn to get along by yourself much of the time."

"By myself? You mean, all alone in the wilderness?"

"Well…" Sadie paused to consider. "…well, yes. Our cousins Fina and Lena have houses on either side of Eli's place, maybe only a quarter-mile in either direction. Still, if something were to happen, they're too far away to hear you scream inside your house."

Pleasant paled. "*Scream?* Are you talking about outlaws?"

"Yes, I am." Sadie exchanged a quick look with Belle. "Among other things. But we're going to teach you how to defend yourself against them."

"Oh my word!" Pleasant said, and felt a sudden nausea creep into her stomach.

"NO!"

Pleasant pulled herself up straight at Honoria's bark. "What?"

Honoria pointed a finger at her. "No, I said. You will *not* faint!"

Sadie opened her mouth as if to scold her daughter,

then stopped and turned back to Pleasant. "She could have been more…diplomatic, but Honoria's right. That fainting business needs to stop."

"Of course." Pleasant took a shuddering breath and did her best to steel herself. The upside to having six older brothers was that she'd always had plenty of protection—and if they weren't around, her father or the servants certainly were. She realized she had never been alone before, had never had to be self-reliant. But now she did, and that left no room for swooning spells.

She had to stand—and stay standing—on her own two feet here. And the thought scared her to death.

"So how's yer place look?" Tom asked Eli as he came into the sheriff's office later that day.

"Looks fine. The women did a wonderful job cleanin' it up. I dunno how I'm gonna thank 'em."

"I think what we got locked up in them cells in the back is thanks enough, li'l brother. We're gonna have to transport 'em to Oregon City, though."

Eli's eyes widened. "But Tom, my bride just got here. I ain't even had a chance to court her yet!"

"Don't worry, I'll have Henry ask Anson if he can help transport 'em."

"Ain't the judge comin'?" Eli asked.

"'Course he is, but we got these varmints dead to rights, so they'll still hafta go to Oregon City jail eventually. And there's a good chance we'll be the ones to take 'em."

"That'll be an awful long time for Anson to be away. Besides, he ain't no deputy, Tom. Not officially anyways."

"I'll have to deputize him so he can do it. Otherwise, you'll hafta, and that'll take ya away from Miss Comfort."

"True 'nough," Eli agreed. "But I gotta bad feelin' about Anson and Henry escortin' a wagonload of prisoners all that way."

"Well, let's see what the judge says when he comes," Tom suggested. "Maybe he'll order someone else to do it. Or just hang 'em," he added, his voice louder so as to carry back to the cells in the back. That wasn't likely, but it never hurt to put a scare into the prisoners.

Eli glanced at the door leading to the cells. "One of 'em's awful young. I'd hate to see him hafta go to Oregon City. Or…" He pantomimed hanging from a noose.

"I know which one yer talkin' 'bout. How's his horse?"

"I took her over to Anson and Emeline's—they've got more room than Chase does. The boy was right— that mare's a nice horse. She oughta foal in 'bout a month."

Tom nodded but said nothing. They both knew the boy could well stand trial along with his older brother— it all depended on how merciful the judge was that day. Not to mention the state of his stomach. Judge Henry Whipple had a wide circuit and would normally head to Portland, then travel up and across the Washington Territory to the town of Nowhere, south from there through Clear Creek and back to Oregon City.

He'd dealt with Judge Whipple the previous year, when he was a deputy in Nowhere in the Washington Territory. Daniel Weaver had just gotten married, and some fellow by the name of Stanley had accosted his wife. What a fiasco that was—not helped a whit by the judge's persistent indigestion. And this time, because of the outlaws they'd captured, he'd have to do the route backwards and come to Clear Creek sooner than normal. It wouldn't be likely to improve Whipple's mood.

"Well, if'n ya have things under control here, I'd best be off," Eli said.

"Ya headin' out to the Triple-C?"

"I thought I'd run by the mercantile first and pick up Miss Comfort a little present," Eli said. "Women like that sort of thing, ya know."

Tom laughed. "Yer ears are turnin' pink, brother. Ain't no shame in buyin' her a present."

Eli smiled and put on his hat. "No, I guess there ain't. It's just this is all new to me. You've already been through this. Tell me, did the whole business sour *your* stomach?"

"Some—but only 'cause it looked like Rose would marry Matty Quinn 'stead of me." Tom laughed and shook his head. "And when Rose was carryin' Hannah I felt sick a few times for real. Musta been nerves."

"What about when she was carryin' Silas?"

"Weren't as bad then—I guess 'cause I'd already been through it," Tom explained.

Eli let out a shaky breath. "Maybe I just oughta marry her and get it over with."

"And leave her to her own devices at your place? No sir, I'd let the Cooke women have a go at her first. Yer stomach will thank ya later."

Eli laughed and nodded in agreement. A bad gut was no joke, and a terrible thing to have to deal with when chasing down an outlaw. "See ya tomorrow, brother," he said with a wave of his hand.

When he got to the mercantile, Wilfred was behind the counter. "Just the man I wanted to see," he declared.

"Howdy, Eli," Wilfred greeted. "What can I do for you?"

"I need a present for my bride. Something purty, I think."

"Oh, that Southern belle that was in here yesterday? Mighty pretty gal. How's she holding up?"

"Don't know. I haven't seen her yet today."

"Well, how'd she hold up yesterday?"

"Uh...fine. 'Til she fainted."

"Fainted?" Wilfred said as his eyebrows rose in amusement. "Land sakes, what did you do to her?"

"I didn't do nothin'! 'Cept tell her 'bout...oh. I guess maybe I did."

"You told her about what?" Wilfred asked leaning forward.

"'Bout the outlaws I shot."

"Awww, Eli! You can't tell a lady like her such things. No wonder she swooned!"

"What do ya mean, a lady like her?" Eli asked.

"She's not from around here. Them high-born Southern women are different—they aren't used to getting their hands dirty. Ask your brother about the Davis girls up in Nowhere. Not to mention their mother—she's a real handful."

Eli laughed. "Yeah, Tom's told me 'bout them. I guess ol' Nellie Davis is still workin' at that restaurant on account of her disruptin' a trial."

"Must've been Judge Whipple," Wilfred commented. "Come to think, he ought to be coming to town soon to deal with those outlaws you caught."

"He is. Tom and I were just talkin' 'bout it. But forget about him—I need a present."

"Well, let me see...how about a box of candy?"

"That might be nice, so long as I don't eat it on my way to the Triple-C. What else ya got?"

Wilfred clasped his hands behind his back and began to pace behind the counter. "It's gotta be something pretty and romantic," he mused. He snapped his fingers and spun to face Eli. "I've got it!"

"Got what?"

"The perfect romantic present. At least for around here."

"Don't keep me in suspense. What is it?"

"It's a couple of things, actually. One is in the back—come on, I'll show you."

Eli smiled. Everyone in town knew Wilfred was a hopeless romantic, so any suggestion he made had to be good. He just hoped his future bride thought so too.

Chapter Eight

Pleasant flopped onto her bed and wiped the sweat off her brow. Never in her life had she worked so hard—and all she'd done was bake! Who knew bread could be so tough to make or cookies so intricate? Never mind about the cake—that was a total disaster from start to finish. No wonder her father kept a cook, or sometimes two…

"Supper is in a half-hour!" Belle called through her door. "Eli will be here!"

"Eli?" Pleasant whispered to herself. "Oh yes—Mr. Turner." She'd almost forgotten about him, the root cause of all this drudgery. If that was baking, what was laundry going to be like? It would do her in for sure.

She groaned in pain as she got up and went to the armoire. She would have to dress for dinner, especially if Mr. Turner was to be in attendance. She wished she'd had time for a bath, as she was covered in sweat. But that wasn't about to happen. The best she could hope for was to wash off some of the grime with what she had at hand.

She went to the washstand and was cleaning up as

best she could when Honoria entered the room. "Are you excited about seeing Mr. Turner again?" the girl asked.

Pleasant stared at her with tired eyes. "Pray I don't fall asleep at the table."

Honoria laughed. "Oh dear. Did we wear you out?"

"I'm not used to such…vigorous activities in the kitchen. Do you do this every day?"

"No, only for special occasions. We usually bake about half as much."

"Well, I'm certainly glad I'll be in a household with only one man to take care of. That should cut the work down considerably."

"Of that I'm certain," Honoria said with a smile, then sighed.

"What's the matter?" Pleasant asked. Did she really look that bad? Maybe she *should* take a bath.

"Nothing. I'm just happy that you're marrying Eli."

"Oh," Pleasant said in surprise. "Um, thank you. You're hoping to get married one day, aren't you?"

"Of course I am. If a gentleman ever comes along that I want to marry. But that's not likely to happen around here, and it's not as if I can send away for a mail-order husband."

"No, I suppose not." Pleasant dried her hands. "But don't worry—you'll get married one day."

"One day," Honoria echoed with a far-off look in her eye.

Pleasant smiled. She couldn't imagine what it would be like to be in a small town with no prospects. How many years would it be before the poor girl finally got a husband? Maybe her family would send her to stay with relatives in a more populous place. But from the sounds of it, that might mean England. She could tell that Honoria loved her family very much—too much to travel a continent and an ocean away. "I suppose it's time to dress for dinner."

"Why?" Honoria asked. "Why change your clothes just to have supper?"

"I always have. It's just the way I was brought up."

"Around here, there's no reason for it," Honoria said. "Why did you do it where you come from?"

"Well, to look nice for…er, to look nice. One wants to always look their best."

"I'd like to hear you say that after a day of laundry. Two or three days, actually."

Pleasant swallowed hard. "You mean it takes two to three days just to do *laundry*?"

"Around here it does."

"Oh dear me," Pleasant whispered. Yes, thank heavens she'd only have one man to take care of!

"Laundry day is tomorrow, by the way," Honoria said with a little smirk.

"I declare, are you enjoying my discomfort, Miss Cooke?" She didn't think the girl was being malicious, but decided to ask.

"Not at all—though I guess it's funny that you're such a 'greenhorn.' You'll learn, though. And if we didn't care, we wouldn't be teaching you."

Pleasant sighed and wiped her hands on her skirt. "I can't thank you enough for doing so. Your mother and aunt are very kind. If not for them, I would be going into this marriage without an ounce of experience."

"That's something we wouldn't wish on anyone, not around these parts. Just try to learn all that you can before you marry Eli. He'll appreciate it and so will you."

Pleasant felt the hot sting of tears. Maybe it was because she was so exhausted, or that she realized the kindness these women were showing her. They didn't have to teach her anything, let alone take her into their home until she married. Before she could think, she stepped over to Honoria and hugged her. "Thank you so much for all your help."

Honoria gently pushed them apart. "It's our pleasure, Miss Comfort. Now let's get ready for supper."

Eli tethered his horse to the hitching post in front of the main ranch house at the Triple-C. He dismounted and then dug through his saddlebags for the gifts he'd brought for Miss Comfort. He ran a hand through his hair, ascended the porch steps and went to the front door, then took a few deep breaths before knocking.

"Well, if it isn't the groom," Colin said as he opened the door and motioned him inside. "Pray tell, what's in the box?"

Eli looked at the box in his hands. "A gift for Miss Comfort. Several, actually."

Colin grinned. "Did Wilfred help you pick them out?"

"He didn't help—he did everythin' himself," Eli confessed.

Colin laughed. "That's Wilfred for you. What did he choose?"

Eli held the box away from him. "I ain't tellin' you or nobody else. Ya'll find out when Miss Comfort does."

Colin laughed again and slapped him on the back. "Very well, but Harrison is going to have a hard time waiting. He's worse than I am when it comes to surprises."

"So I've heard," Eli said with an arched eyebrow.

Of the three Cooke brothers, it was well known around Clear Creek that Harrison was the most easily flustered. He might have to hide the box from Harrison entirely.

They went into the dining parlor, and Eli set the box on a chair against the wall. He peeked around for any sign of Harrison, then took off his coat and covered the box with it. "There, that oughta keep it safe."

Colin laughed and motioned for Eli to follow him into the kitchen. "Is supper almost ready, sweet?" Colin asked Belle. "Our company has arrived."

"Eli," she said with a smile as she turned, handing a bowl of mashed potatoes to Colin. "Here, put this on the table. And Eli can carry this in." She picked up a platter of chicken and held it before him. "Provided your hands are steady enough. If I didn't know any better, I'd say you were nervous."

"What…what makes ya say that, ma'am?" he asked.

"For one, you've never called me 'ma'am' before. It's always been 'Belle'."

He noticed his breathing was a little faster than normal. Land sakes, she was right—he *was* nervous. "Well, maybe just a bit…"

"He's come to bestow a gift upon his intended," Colin informed her. "A box containing who knows what treasures?"

"Oh, I see," Belle said with glee. "Did Uncle Wilfred help you pick something out?"

"Wilfred did all the picking, dear," Colin informed her before Eli could.

"Oh, I can't wait to see what it is!"

Eli's face twisted up into a grimace. "Don't I get a li'l credit? Listenin' to you two makes me think I just put all my romantic notions in Wilfred's hands. I did have some say."

"Of course you did," Belle said. "But my uncle does like to have his hand in it." She hefted a bowl of vegetables. "Let's take these to the table, then come back for the rest."

"What else is there?" Colin asked.

"I still have to slice the bread, and put the corn on a plate."

"I say," Colin mused, "but didn't our house guest help with the meal preparation?" He winked at Eli.

"Only the bread. Though she certainly had her hand in dessert."

"You mean our dear Mr. Turner will have a chance to taste her cooking?" Colin teased.

"Her baking, and yes, come dessert time. Now go put the food on the table!"

Colin chuckled as he complied, leading the trio into the dining room. They placed everything on the table, then went back for more food as the family began to gather.

Eli felt himself getting nervous. Where was Miss Comfort? He edged his way into the foyer and glanced up the staircase, just in time to see his intended and Honoria come out of one of the bedrooms. He heard a funny sound…and realized he had gasped!

And with reason—Miss Comfort was stunning in a pink gown the likes of which he'd never seen before. She looked like a storybook princess. Honoria followed in her Sunday best. The two women were beautiful, and he had a momentary pang of regret at not taking a chance on Harrison and Sadie's daughter. After all, it would've been easy to marry someone he already knew. But he also knew they would never have suited.

"Good evening, Mr. Turner," his bride greeted him as she reached the bottom of the stairs.

Eli gawked. "Good evenin'. Ya, ya look…tarnation! I dunno how to describe ya."

"Beautiful?" Honoria suggested from behind her, smirking as she so often did.

Eli nodded, still too dumbstruck to talk properly. He couldn't believe he would be married to this vision soon.

Honoria giggled, shook her head and made her way past them both. Miss Comfort stood on the last step, which put her at eye level with him. "I'm happy to see you again, Mr. Turner," she said softly.

A shiver ran up his spine and he swallowed hard. "Me too, ma'am. I mean… I'm happy to see ya."

She smiled. "I understood what you meant. Shall we go into the dining room?"

"Uh-huh," he said, never taking his eyes off of her.

"Then that means we'll have to walk there," she pointed out.

"Oh. Yeah." He took a step back. "Plumb forgot about that part."

She smiled as her shoulders shook with silent laughter. Lord help him, but he'd already managed to make a fool of himself, and they hadn't even sat down to supper yet. He offered her his arm. "May I escort ya in?"

Her smile softened, and she wrapped her arm around his. "Thank you."

Eli's heart swelled at the contact. Never had he seen such a beautiful woman. And to think she would be his, every last lovely inch. So what if she couldn't cook or sew or clean yet? At the moment, he didn't care…

though maybe one good bellyache would cure that. He smiled as he set the thought aside and escorted his future bride to dinner.

The meal was quite pleasant, the food wonderful—especially the bread. At least Eli thought so. If his bride could bake bread this well, what else could she do? He couldn't wait to find out.

He also couldn't wait to give Miss Comfort her gifts. Thankfully, the meal was winding down. He planned on having dessert with her on the front porch. It was a nice evening, not too cool, perfect for courting a beautiful lady…

Eli shook himself. Great Scott, he was beginning to sound like Wilfred!

"Is there anything wrong, Mr. Turner?" his vision of loveliness asked.

"Not at all," he said, his voice cracking. He cleared his throat. "Would you like to have dessert on the porch with me, Miss Comfort?" He caught the quick glance Harrison and Sadie exchanged. "I hope the Cookes won't mind if I deprive 'em of your company for a while."

Belle smiled. "We don't mind at all. Do we, Colin?"

Colin shook his head. "No, not us."

Eli smiled. They, of course, knew about the box. Harrison and Sadie, on the other hand, didn't. He looked at them, his smile frozen in place.

"Well, that would be fine," Sadie slowly agreed. "We can have our dessert and coffee in the parlor while the two of you…retire to the porch."

Colin pushed his chair from the table and stood. "Shall we see to dessert, my sweet?"

"Certainly," Belle said brightly.

Colin grinned at Harrison and Sadie, then followed Belle into the kitchen.

Harrison glanced around the table. "What was that all about?"

"I haven't the slightest idea." Sadie gave Eli a quizzical look.

He shrugged innocently. "Miss Comfort, are you ready?"

She daintily wiped her mouth and set her napkin on the table. "Of course."

Now Harrison was looking suspicious. Eli had to move carefully. He walked around the table and offered his arm to Miss Comfort, who took it with ease. He could get used to this. He escorted her from the room, swung by the chair holding his coat and whisked the box out from under it.

"What's that?" Harrison asked.

Eli, too nervous to bluff his way through it, settled for ignoring him.

Harrison's mouth dropped open, and he quickly turned to his wife. "He brought something for her and didn't tell us!"

Sadie smiled and shook her head. "Really, Harrison, do mind your own business. Whatever it is, he didn't bring it for *you*."

"But he didn't tell us!"

"So?" She got up from the table. "Help me with these dishes so we can have dessert."

"But they've gone out onto the porch, dear wife. You know what that means."

"I can't say that I do." She began to clear away the plates.

"Where is your sense of snoopery?" he asked indignantly.

"Snoopery? What kind of word is that?"

"I just made it up. If you will excuse me…" He moved to leave the room.

Sadie set down the stack of plates in her hands and followed him into the parlor. She watched as he quickly opened the front window, the one that looked out over the porch. Eli's and Miss Comfort's voices drifted into the room. "Harrison Cooke!" she hissed. "Get away from that window!"

He went to her and took her hands in his. "It's our duty, dear wife, to chaperone. Now what kind of chaperones would we be if we left them alone out there, unwatched and unlistened to?"

"Oh for Heaven's sake." Sadie yanked her hands from his. "You are the nosiest man I have ever met!"

"On the contrary," he said in a low voice. "I'm doing what's right by Miss Comfort and our young friend Mr. Turner."

Sadie put her hands on her hips. "You just want to see what's in the box."

"A nice side benefit," he admitted, waving a finger at her. "But making sure it is nothing untoward, of course."

Sadie rolled her eyes. "Harrison, you've gone plumb loco." She left to deal with the dirty dishes.

"That woman has no sense of romance," he muttered. Harrison turned, rubbed his hands together in anticipation, then firmly planted himself in the chair next to the open window.

Chapter Nine

"I brought ya somethin'." Eli handed her a box.

"Why, Mr. Turner," Pleasant said with a smile. "A gift? For me?"

"I hope ya like it," he said nervously.

What she liked was the way the tips of his ears turned pink. It was an odd thing to notice and even odder to be attracted to, but there it was. She took the box from him and stared at it. It was a little larger than a shoebox, wrapped in brown paper and string. "You really didn't have to get me anything."

"I wanted to." He gazed into her eyes. "Besides, they're real practical. Stuff ya'd be needin' anyways."

"How very thoughtful." She tugged on the string, untied it, pulled the paper away and opened the box. "Oh my…what is all this?"

"That li'l box there." Eli pointed at it. "It's got somethin' else in it."

"Indeed?" She felt herself blush. For a man who'd just shot several outlaws the day before, he was acting incredibly nervous, boyish and innocent at the same time. What a startling contrast—how could a man be so manly and tough, yet tender and charming? Pleasant found she liked the combination. She liked it a lot. "What's this?" she asked, picking up an object wrapped in white linen. "It's heavy…"

"Careful, now," he warned. "I'll hafta teach ya how to use it."

She pulled the linen away and… "Merciful heavens!" she gasped, a hand to her chest. It was a pearl-handled revolver!

"Ya'll need some lessons. I'll teach ya how to load it first. Then ya can try yer hand at shootin' it."

She examined the weapon and almost dropped it from her shaking hands. "But I've… I've never shot a gun in my life!"

"If'n yer married to me, yer gonna hafta learn," he said, his voice stern. "I don't mean for it to scare ya, I'm just tryin' to make sure yer safe."

She knew the gun couldn't possibly be loaded… could it? Gingerly she set it in her lap. "Protect me? By having *me* shoot someone?"

"Only if ya gotta." He took the gun from her and aimed it at the barn. "Mr. Dunnigan—ya know, Wilfred? He just got it in—says it's a perfect sidearm for a lady, nice and light. And it's real purty, don't ya think?"

"Yes, it's…quite beautiful. I've never seen anything like it." As a child near the end of the War, when Sherman's army came stomping through Savannah, she remembered a few ladies carrying firearms. But those were tiny things, little two-shot pistols you could fit in your reticule. This six-shooter was a whole other animal!

"Wilfred thought ya'd like this, and I agreed. It might seem a little heavy at first, but you'll get used to it."

She nodded and swallowed hard. Right now it was pretty, with its pearl handle and shiny steel. But what would it be like to actually fire the thing? She didn't ask and instead picked up the small box inside the larger one. "What about this?"

"Open it and find out," he said with a smile.

She was almost afraid to after the gun—did this contain the bullets? But she pressed on…and was glad she did. "Mr. Turner, are these truffles?"

"Yes, ma'am," he said with obvious pride. "Came all the way from Oregon City."

"How delightful!" The rich fungi brought back memories of her debutante ball, where her father—who was still spending money like he had it—had served truffles shipped all the way from France. It was one of her last completely fond recollections of home…

"There's somethin' else in there if'n ya look for it," Eli said, still smiling.

She smiled back, feeling positively giddy. She looked again into the box and saw a small piece of cloth folded into a square. She picked it up and felt something inside.

"Go ahead," he urged. "Open it."

She did and pulled out a lovely silver necklace. "Oh, Mr. Turner! You shouldn't have." She looked at the truffles and the gun. "I can see where the gun will come in handy, but these other things are great extravagances, are they not?" Good heavens, did she actually say that? Back home, such things would be expected from a suitor. But out here, days from the nearest city, such luxuries were just that—luxuries.

"Shucks, Miss Comfort. I know ya'll need the gun. But what woman doesn't like tasty treats? And the necklace'll look mighty purty on ya."

She almost sobbed in happiness. She'd had men in Savannah flirt with her before and offer such trinkets, even try to steal a kiss from her when her brothers weren't around. (Pity the poor fellow once they found out, of course.) But never had any man caught her eye as this one was doing now. A good thing too, considering she was supposed to marry him. "Thank you. Thank you so much. Though I will admit that this one token does fret me something awful." She carefully tapped the butt of the gun with a finger.

"Ya mean that li'l thing?" He picked up the gun again. "It won't be so scary once ya know how to use it. In fact, it'll be downright comfortin', I bet." He grinned. "Comfort. If'n ya don't mind my sayin' so, that's quite a name. I've never heard it before."

She sighed. They were bound to get around to this. "Oh, it's much worse than that."

"I never said it was bad."

"No, but you will when you hear the rest of it."

His eyebrows rose at that. "So…yer full name is?"

"Pleasant. Anne. Comfort."

"P-P-Pleasant? Your name is *Pleasant*?" He laughed and slapped his leg with a hand. "Well, I'll be! If that ain't the purtiest name I ever did hear!"

She looked at him in shock. "Pretty? You think it's *pretty*?"

"Yes, ma'am, I do. As purty as the girl wearin' it."

Pleasant felt herself blush as she put the necklace back in the box. "I don't know what to say. I've always been ashamed of my name."

"Ashamed? Why? I think it's beautiful."

"After I marry you, I won't be wearing it anymore—

or at least, not part of it. I'll be Pleasant Turner. Thankfully, there's not much one can do with that."

"What do ya mean?" he asked, confused.

She sighed. "What I mean is that children can be very cruel and were, when I grew up. Of course, some of my brothers dealt with even worse than I did."

"Why, what are their names?"

"My oldest brother's name is Major."

She watched as Eli closed his eyes a moment. "Major Comfort?"

"Mm-hmm. And my twin brother, a few minutes older than I am, is named Peaceful."

Eli's eyes sprang open in horror. "Now 'round here, if'n someone's daddy named 'em somethin' like that, they'd get a talkin' to!"

She nodded. "Mother could be…eccentric about such things. As I said, Peaceful had a much harder time of it than I ever did. He still does—that's why we'll call him Matt. From Matthias, his middle name."

"What about your older brother, Major?" Eli asked, shaking his head.

"We call him Quince for short. His middle name is Quincy."

"Quincy sounds kinda…well, sissy to me. If'n ya don't mind my sayin'," he added defensively.

"Well, I warn you that if you ever meet him, don't tell him that. He *would* mind your saying, trust me."

He nodded. "I'll take yer word for it." He put the gun back in the box and reached for her hand. "May I?"

She looked at him in confusion. "May you what?"

He smiled as he took the necklace from her. "Put this on ya?"

"Oh yes, of course." She turned on the swing to make

it easier for him. He drew closer as he brought the neck-lace up and over her head, then pinned it at the back of her neck brushing a few wisps of hair away in the process. She shuddered at his touch and quickly turned back to him. "How does it look?"

He smiled. "Beautiful." His eyes drifted up to meet hers. "'Course, I think anythin' would look purty on you, Pleasant. Ya don't mind if I use yer first name, do ya?"

"Well, it's a little soon…but we are going to be married, aren't we?"

"We sure 'nough are." He drew closer.

Pleasant's eyes darted to his lips. Good heavens, was she thinking of kissing him? How scandalous would that be? But this wasn't Savannah—would it actually be a scandal here? And he did have nice lips…

"Here you are!" Harrison stomped out onto the porch, making them both jump. "Oh, I'm terribly sorry—I didn't mean to startle you. I was just bringing dessert."

Eli let out the breath he'd been holding. "Much obliged," he said sourly.

Harrison gave them a toothy grin and set a tray on a small table near the swing. "Coffee, and pie baked by our own Miss Comfort."

Eli's face lit up. "Ya baked a pie?"

"I went through the motions. Belle told me what to do, step-by-step."

"But it was still yer hands that made it."

"He's right, you know," Harrison tossed in. "Take credit for your achievement, Miss Comfort." His eyes fixed on the box in her lap. "Oh, what have we here?"

"Mr. Turner was kind enough to bestow upon me a few gifts," she said.

He eyed the gun. "How…practical of him." He turned

to Eli. "You'd better be sure you have Doc Drake with you when you teach her how to use it."

Eli looked taken aback. "I ain't gonna let her get hurt, Harrison! She won't need Doc!"

"I wasn't talking about *her* getting hurt." He spun on his heel and headed back into the house.

Pleasant put a hand over her mouth to stifle a giggle. "What's so funny?" Eli asked.

"Nothing," she said with a shake of her head. "Except that I think he's right."

"About what?"

"About having the doctor present when you teach me how to use that. I'm liable to shoot your foot off."

His eyes widened. "Ya *are*?"

"I'm afraid so. I've never shot a pistol, but I have used a bow and arrow. And I have terrible aim."

He looked away, swallowed hard, then met her gaze once more. "Okay, I'll ask Doc Drake what he's up to this week." He smiled. "Now let's see how this pie tastes, shall we?"

Pleasant laughed, nodded, then realized how much fun she was having.

She sighed as Eli took his first bite. He chewed slowly, his eyes wandering. When he finally turned back to her, Pleasant's chest swelled with pride at the look of pleasure on his face. "Do you like it?"

"Darlin', if'n this is yer very first pie, I can't imagine what the hundredth is gonna be like. Maybe I should marry ya tomorrow."

Pleasant blushed. She was inclined to agree.

Pleasant awoke the next morning with renewed hope. This mail-order bride business might work out after all.

She liked Eli Turner and was looking forward to getting to know him better.

Unfortunately, she didn't get to see much of him over the next few days because of his job. But how often did the town jail hold a passel of outlaws awaiting the circuit judge? Not very, according to Sadie. Still, the town had seen its share of things since she'd married Harrison all those years ago, so this wouldn't be the last time. Pleasant would have to get used to being the wife of a lawman.

She wanted to meet Eli's brother, the sheriff, and his wife. If anyone would know what it was like being married to one, it would be Rose Turner. She and Tom, Colin informed her, had married six years ago, when Tom was deputy in a town called (believe it or not) *Nowhere*, up in Washington Territory. They had two children and did fine, according to Colin and Harrison.

But the lifestyle of a small-town sheriff was far from the only thing she'd have to get used to. Common housework was another—cooking, cleaning, sewing, laundry. And feeding animals—did Eli have any besides his horse? She certainly hoped he didn't keep pigs. What if he had some beasts she was allergic to? Did he have a cat? She certainly hoped so. She hated mice and rats—they scared her to death. But she hadn't noticed any vermin at the Triple-C so far, and that was a good sign. Though she hadn't seen a cat there—maybe the Cookes kept one in the barn...

What she most wanted to see wasn't a cat, though—it was Eli. Belle informed her that this was his day off, and the timing was perfect—she and Sadie were going to town for some sort of sewing circle, and planned to visit Mr. Turner at his home. At last she would see where she would live. She envisioned a pretty little two-story house with flower boxes and a garden…

The words *one-room cabin* flashed in her mind, dispelling the fantasy. She'd forgotten about the description. Still, she could hardly wait to see what it was like. It might be a *nice* one-room cabin, after all.

"Are you ladies ready yet?" Colin asked as Sadie, Belle and Pleasant came downstairs. "We've got the wagon all hitched up."

"Yes, we're ready," Belle said.

He kissed her on the cheek. "Are you ready, Miss Comfort? After all, this is going to be a big day for you."

She glanced at each in turn. "How so? I am looking forward to seeing Mr. Turner's home, but…"

Belle cleared her throat as Colin began to study the ceiling. Sadie glared at both of them, then turned to her. "He's talking about the ladies' sewing circle. You'll get to meet quite a few of the women in town."

"Oh?" Pleasant said. "My, I had no idea so many attended."

"It's not saying much," Belle said. "Clear Creek isn't that big."

"So I'll get to meet a good percentage of them," Pleasant commented with a smile, and Belle chuckled.

Harrison walked in through the front door and did a quick head count. "Honoria!" he called up the stairs. "Come along, sweetling, or we'll be late."

"I'm coming." She hurried down to join them, adjusted her bonnet, smiled at her parents, then rushed out the door before anyone had a chance to blink.

"I declare," Pleasant said. "But what's her hurry?"

"Her father hates being late," Sadie explained.

"Quite so," Harrison agreed, offering Sadie his arm. "Shall we to town then, wife?"

She smiled before wrapping her arm through his. "We shall." Colin followed suit, and Belle took his arm with a bright smile.

Pleasant watched the two couples and felt a pinch of envy. She wondered if Mr. Turner had such manners tucked away somewhere. From what she'd seen so far, he was far rougher. But was it fair to compare him to the Cookes? They were English gentlemen and their manners had not been dampened by years living in the American West. She, born and raised on a Southern plantation, had also been taught impeccable manners.

She hoped she'd be able to keep hers intact after years of marriage to a farm-raised country lawman. Yet he'd been so utterly charming and—dare she say— adorable the night he'd presented her with her gifts. He was hardly without dignity or grace.

She smiled at the thought and followed her hosts out the door.

By the time they got to town she'd convinced herself once again that she was doing the right thing, that Mr. Turner was a good choice for her. Not to mention the only choice, as far as Mrs. Pettigrew was concerned. Pleasant suspected she had other applicants, but for some reason the woman was adamant that Mr. Turner was the right one. She'd put her trust in the matchmaker, as had her aunt. Best to hold onto that and hope the woman knew what she was doing.

"Here we are!" Harrison announced as he brought the team to a halt in front of Dunnigan's Mercantile.

"Have a good time, ladies. Colin and I will tend to our business while you tend to yours."

"Business?" Sadie said with a huff. "You're going to the sheriff's office to see if Tom got a letter from Sheriff Hughes."

"Harlan Hughes, dearest," Harrison said. "He's retired, remember?"

"To me he'll always be Sheriff Hughes," she said.

"Harlan's sister Leona lives in Nowhere, Washington," Belle explained to Pleasant. "He married a widow, Mary Weaver, a mother of four sons. All four are married now, with *lots* of children, living together on a huge farm. Getting a letter from Harlan and listening to Tom—Sheriff Turner—read about the things that happen up there keeps us entertained for weeks!"

Pleasant smiled, confused. "You have a large family with lots of children on your place. What's the difference?"

Colin and Harrison exchanged a quick glance. "Because these are *Weavers*," Colin said, in a voice to strike terror into the soul.

"The Weavers are a, er…boisterous lot," Harrison said.

"To put it diplomatically," Sadie added dryly. "Sheriff Turner can tell you all about them."

"And where our families combined are formidable, we're much more, shall we say, birds of a feather?" Colin said. "The Weaver men married women from all over."

"All over where?" Pleasant asked him as he helped Belle out of the wagon.

"One is from the South like yourself," he said. "One

came from back East somewhere—Connecticut, I think. Another is Italian and yet another is Swedish."

"What's so odd about that?" she asked. It sounded like a typically diverse day at the port of Savannah to her.

"Oh, and the Italian woman brought her seven younger brothers and sisters to live with them," Harrison mentioned as he helped Sadie down.

Pleasant's eyes went wide. "*Seven?*"

"Seven *Italian* children," Harrison emphasized. "All of them loud. We number at twenty if you count the Kincaids but not the ranch hands. They're at twenty-five…twenty-six…somewhere around there."

Pleasant could only stare. "This Harlan fellow must write quite a letter."

"Every time!" Harrison helped her down.

Once she was on her feet she began to fan herself with her hand. "Oh dear. I've never given any thought to children." She stared at them, wide-eyed. "I do hope Mr. Turner isn't expecting me to bear him an army!"

The two couples looked at one another, then burst out laughing.

"I see nothing funny about it!" Pleasant took a few steps back. "Really!"

Belle managed to calm down first. "I think you'd best take things one step at a time, Miss Comfort. Worry about getting married first."

Pleasant absently smoothed her skirt and patted her hair, feeling her cheeks grow hot. "Yes, of course." There was nothing worse than making a fool of herself in public. She shouldn't have said anything, but in her panic—not to mention a vision of herself with twelve little ones running willy-nilly—she'd spoken before thinking. She really needed to collect herself.

"Shall we go inside?" Sadie asked as she, too, stifled her chuckles.

"Yes, let's." Pleasant practically ran up the mercantile's front steps. The sooner she could get away from the subject of children, the better!

Chapter Ten

"Why, she had fourteen children at last count!" Fanny Fig stated as if it were nothing.

Pleasant sat, horrified at the tale. No one of her acquaintance had that many children, or even close.

"I wouldn't mind another one," Lena Adams replied and looked at Pleasant. "Then he or she could play with your children."

Pleasant looked around the room at the gathered ladies. It was a small group this week, so they met in the mercantile. When most of the women were in attendance, they met at the church. Still, there were over a dozen, most of them English and related to the Cookes.

"Promise me you'll let Lena and I help you put in a garden," Fina Stone, Lena's sister, said.

Pleasant would be thoroughly shocked if she remembered all their names. The two who'd just spoken, however, were the more important—they were Mr. Turner's neighbors, each living on either side of him. Not right next door, mind you, but near enough by Clear Creek standards. Lena explained she wouldn't be able to see either house from Mr. Turner's, but they were both within a reasonable walking distance.

"Certainly, that would be lovely," she said. She'd never tended a garden in her life. One more thing to learn.

"I don't believe Eli has spoken to my husband yet," said Annie King, the town preacher's wife. "Do you plan to marry soon?"

"I'm not quite sure what Mr. Turner's exact plans are," Pleasant answered.

"Miss Comfort, I adore you name!" a blonde woman said. Another Cooke cousin, one named after a fruit. Pear? Plum?

"Why, thank you," Pleasant said for safety's sake.

"Are we gonna make this poor woman a wedding dress or not?" Irene Dunnigan barked, making everyone jump.

"Yes, of course, Auntie," Belle said. "And as soon as it's done, Pleasant and Eli can be married."

Pleasant smiled. These women were nothing like the sour old matrons of Savannah. Some of the older ones looked a little careworn, but were—save for Mrs. Dunnigan—still cheerful. Mrs. Waller, the doctor's wife whom everyone called "Grandma," was the oldest— she had to be approaching her eighties, but could still giggle like a schoolgirl.

"Why don't you have a wedding dress if you came here to be married?" the fruit—Apple, that was her name!—asked.

Pleasant straightened in her chair. She couldn't tell them it was because she'd stolen away like a thief in the night to avoid marrying Rupert Jerney. "I didn't have time to get one." Which was true. "The matchmaker said I'd have to leave immediately."

"That's strange," commented Annie. "I don't recall Eli being in a hurry."

Pleasant glanced around the room. "Perhaps she had other brides whom might have taken Mr. Turner. I'm not sure."

"Is there much competition?" Mary Mulligan asked in her Irish brogue. "Are the men that scarce where ye come from?"

Pleasant arched an eyebrow. "Actually, they are somewhat. The war…"

"We don't discuss politics here!" Irene huffed.

"You're just bitter the Rebs lost," Fanny carped.

"Fanny!" Annie said, aghast.

"And now you know why we don't discuss politics," Sadie muttered in Pleasant's ear.

Irene's face was red as a tomato as she glared at Pleasant. "Do you want a dress or not?"

Pleasant's mouth dropped open. "My word!"

"Auntie," Belle interjected. "Of course she does." She turned to Pleasant. "We can all pitch in and have you a dress in no time."

"Oh, but if it's a bother…"

"Nonsense, we'd love to!" Grandma Waller said. "If you're gonna be a part of this town, you gotta learn how we take care of each other."

Pleasant smiled. "Thank you, Mrs. Waller."

"Call me Grandma. Everyone does."

"I love your accent too!" Apple blurted. Lena rolled her eyes.

Pleasant's eyebrows shot up. One moment she felt as if she were in polite society, surrounded by English ladies. Yet those same ladies were just as quirky as the American-born residents. How long would it take before she began to lose herself in this wilderness? Was it going to be worth it in the long run? Maybe she should've reconsidered…but it was too late for that now.

"Then it's settled!" Irene got up and waddled to a shelf with bolts of fabric. "White or ivory? What's your pleasure?"

All the ladies leaned forward in their seats, awaiting Pleasant's answer. She glanced between them nervously. "White?"

"Good choice!" Irene pulled a bolt of white lace off the shelf, followed by one of white satin. "Let's get to it!"

The women all began talking at once, their suggestions flying every which way. Pleasant fought the urge to cover her ears.

"Quiet!" Grandma yelled as she stood. "Land sakes, I know it's been a while since we had us a wedding around here, but you don't have to go plumb loony! Let Miss Comfort tell us what she wants!"

The women sat like scolded schoolgirls as Grandma retook her seat. Pleasant sank a little in her own chair. For an old woman, Grandma could probably have scared the trousers off General Lee himself.

"Well, Miss Comfort?" Grandma asked. "Tell us what you'd like and we'll do our best to make it for you."

Pleasant swallowed hard. "Well, I…hadn't given my dress much thought until now. I planned on getting married in one of the dresses I brought. This is so kind of you." She glanced around the circle of ladies. "All of you."

"What do you think Eli will like?" Apple asked.

"I have no idea."

"Eli isn't like his brother Tom," another pretty blonde mused. Pleasant couldn't remember her name, only that she was married to the younger doctor in town. Grandma was married to the older one. "I think something simple yet elegant. I should add that no matter what we make, Miss Comfort, with her beauty, will look stunning in it."

Pleasant felt herself blush. "Thank you."

"You have lovely hair," Apple said. "I always wanted to have dark hair like that."

"Stop it—you're fine as you are," a redhead said, speaking up for the first time.

"Oh Penelope, you always say that," Apple said with a roll of her eyes.

"That's because you're always comparing yourself to others," Penelope stated. "Not a good habit."

"Ladies, let's get back to the task at hand," the young doctor's wife said. She turned to Pleasant. "What do you think?"

Pleasant sat, unsure of what to say. She'd never sewn a thing—she'd always gone to a dressmaker's shop for her clothes. Good grief, what if they wanted her to help? "White is fine with me."

"Details, girl, details!" Irene snapped. "How are we supposed to make a wedding dress if you don't tell us what you want? Or would you rather make it yourself?"

"Oh no!" Pleasant said, panicked. "That won't do at all."

"Why not?" Fina asked. "You'd get what you wanted that way."

"Well, I…" Pleasant gulped. "I don't exactly sew

well. Or at all." There, she'd said it. Let them think what they will.

Most of them just shrugged. "Few of us did when we arrived here," Penelope replied. "Few of us knew how to do much of anything." All the Cooke wives and cousins nodded.

Only Fanny Fig seemed shocked. "Don't sew? Land sakes, girl, how old are you?"

"Eighteen," Pleasant told her, more calmly than she felt.

Irene, Mary and Grandma gave each other a sage look. "Where did you say you were from?" Grandma asked.

"I didn't, as I recall," said Pleasant. "Savannah, Georgia."

"Georgia?" Fanny said in shock. "Well, that explains that ridiculous accent, but not why you don't sew!"

"Fanny…" Annie groaned, her face in her hands.

Pleasant was beginning to "lose her religion," as Major liked to say. "I had no reason to learn how to sew where I come from."

"And why is that?" Fanny asked, indignant.

"Because I had a dressmaker and servants, that's why. If I wanted something mended, my maid saw it done."

Several of the women gasped, but not because they felt insulted. "You had servants?" Apple said enviously. "Oh, how I miss having them! I had the most wonderful ladies' maid back in England."

"Well, we had one between the three of us," Fina corrected, then turned to Pleasant. "You were very lucky to have your own."

"Servants?" Mary said with a shake of her head.

"There be none of those here in Clear Creek. As much as it pains me to say, I have to agree with Fanny—ye'll have to learn yer way around a needle, lass. It's fine and dandy ye got to grow up with servants to wait on ye all of yer life, Miss Comfort, but here we make our own way in the world."

"I never said I wouldn't have to learn, Mrs. Mulligan," Pleasant said. "I was simply trying to explain why I haven't yet."

"Land sakes, let's not pick on the poor girl—or anyone else," Grandma said, aiming a glare at Fanny. "We got work to do. We'll take care of your wedding dress for you, Miss Comfort, and we'll gladly teach you how to sew. But eventually you'll have to do it on your own."

"Teach her?" Fanny groused. "Speak for yourself, Grandma."

"Teaching her how to sew is the least ye can do, Fanny!" Mary insisted. "Especially seeing as your husband works with hers."

"And seeing as how you were just treating her," Annie scolded.

All eyes fixed on Fanny, and she sunk lower in her chair. "Fine, I'll pitch in too."

"Mighty neighborly of you, Fanny," Grandma said dryly. She looked at Pleasant. "But as I said, any of us would be glad to help."

Pleasant looked around the circle. "That's one of the nicest things I've ever heard. None of you even know me."

"You're going to marry Eli Turner, ain't ya?" Grandma said. "That makes you a part of this town, and folks around here help each other out—even with sewing lessons. We helped Mrs. Stone and Mrs. Adams and Mrs. Bennett and so on—no reason we wouldn't help you too."

Pleasant smiled. "As I'll be living closest to Mrs. Adams and Mrs. Stone, perhaps they would be willing to help me."

"Of course," Lena said with a smile as Fina nodded vigorously.

Pleasant smiled back. She looked forward to meeting the rest of the English contingent—Penelope's two sisters weren't in attendance that day, partly because, as Belle explained on the way to town, they lived so far away. Penelope's sister Eloise and her husband Seth used to work in the hotel, but turned the job over to another couple, Lorcan and Ada Brody, about five years ago. Ada probably wasn't in attendance because Lorcan was blind and needed her assistance.

"The sooner we get to work on this, ladies, the sooner we get done, and the sooner Miss Comfort can get hitched," Grandma said. She looked at Pleasant. "Now, come on, dear—tell us what you'd like."

Two hours, two plates of cookies and a pitcher of lemonade later, the sewing circle drew to a close. Never had Pleasant been bombarded with so many questions in so short a time—and all over a dress! She'd go over a few with her dressmaker back home, but all she really had to do was tell the woman what color she wanted and the woman did the rest. Here in Clear Creek, things were definitely different—she practically had to tell them where to put each button. And how would she even know where to begin when she'd never sewn before?

But she did come away with a fantastic cookie recipe from Irene. The woman might be cantankerous, but everyone agreed she could cook—half the women in town aspired to the culinary heights of the ladle-wielding grouch. She'd have to ask her for more recipes, if she could work up the nerve.

Pleasant was about to ask Sadie about one other dynamic—Fanny Fig's seeming hostility toward all things Southern—when Eli walked into the mercantile. "Howdy, ladies," he said as his eyes locked on her. "How'd the circle go today?"

"Ye'll be happy to know we're working on yer bride's wedding dress," Mary said with a wink.

"Are ya, now? Well, that suits me fine. How soon do ya think you'll have it done?"

"Next week if things go well," Annie said. "Some of us are meeting at the church tomorrow to work on it. Including your bride," she added with a tiny smile.

Pleasant felt herself blush. "Are you here to buy something, Mr. Turner?" she asked, changing the subject.

"Well, I was in town and thought I'd look at a few things," he said, never taking his eyes off her.

"Seems to me you're looking at only one thing!" Fanny snapped.

"What is in your craw today?" Grandma demanded. "Leave the younguns be! Land sakes, they're gonna get hitched."

"That's no excuse for indecent behavior!" Fanny shot back. Several of the women looked at each other, then at Fanny.

"I assure you, Mrs. Fig," Pleasant said, "that Mr. Turner is doing nothing untoward."

"Of course you'd say that!" Fanny spat. "Otherwise you'd be as guilty as him!"

Now Eli gaped at her, his mouth half-open in shock. "Fanny, what's gotten into ya? I ain't done nothin'! Can't a man look at his bride?"

"Not the way you're looking at her!"

Grandma put her hands on her hips and scowled. "Fanny Fig, if I was Henry, I'd give you a good tongue-lashing the way you're treating these two younguns."

"Well, you're not my Henry, are you? And what's he got to do with any of this anyway?"

"Indeed," Grandma said. "That's what I'd like to know."

Annie wrapped an arm through Fanny's, making the older woman flinch. "Come home with me, Fanny, and you can tell me and Jo all about it."

"Tell you about what? I have nothing to tell!"

"Oh, I think there's plenty," Grandma grabbed Fanny's other arm. The two women escorted her to the door and out the mercantile.

"I declare," Pleasant said, "what is wrong with that woman?"

Mr. Turner shook his head. "Her husband Henry's retirin' soon on account he don't see too good no more. I think it's got poor Fanny all riled up."

"Does the thought of having her husband at home upset her that much?"

"It must. Ever since he told her, she's been nastier'n a polecat to live with, accordin' to Henry. Now I see what he's talkin' 'bout. Ya'd think she'd be happy—it ain't the kind of job where a man's always home for supper."

Pleasant stared at him and felt her heart sink a little. "It's not, is it?"

"No, ma'am. There are times a lawman can be gone for days, even weeks." He flinched at his own words.

"That don't mean I'll have to be gone that long, but sometimes…well, it cain't be helped."

Pleasant slowly nodded. Would she be able to cope with being by herself for days on end without him, or would she go crazy from loneliness? She shook the thought away. For Heaven's sake, why was she even thinking about it? She didn't even know him yet!

"Miss Comfort?"

Pleasant jumped at his voice. "Yes?"

"Would you take a walk with me?"

Chapter Eleven

Eli watched Pleasant look furtively at Sadie and Belle. They each nodded in approval. Did she think they wouldn't let her go with him? He smiled warmly and offered her his arm. "I'd like to show ya the town if'n I may. I got a little time on my hands 'fore the next watch."

"Next watch?"

"Guardin' the prisoners," he explained. "Remember the outlaws we brought in the other day? We cain't do nothin' with 'em 'til Judge Whipple gets to town."

"Oh yes, of course." She wrapped her arm through his. "Lead the way, Mr. Turner."

He escorted her out of the mercantile, crossed the street to the other side and onto the boardwalk. "Now that ya've seen the mercantile, I figgered ya oughta see the rest of Clear Creek."

"You're most kind for showing me, Mr. Turner."

"Well, yer gonna live here, ain't ya?"

"That's the idea."

He smiled, half-gritting his teeth. Every time he was around her, he put his foot in his mouth and made himself look like a fool. He hoped he didn't come across as some dumb country bumpkin. He didn't have much education, just what Mrs. Kincaid had been able to give him and the other kids in town when he was growing up. He could read and write and knew his numbers—what else did you need to get through life?

Besides, the skills he *really needed* to do his job were a lot stronger than his ability to read, write and do sums. Being an excellent horseman and handy with a gun were basic requirements of his trade, not to mention a calm demeanor and the ability to make snap decisions if he had to. Knowing how to throw a good punch helped too.

"Do both doctors live in the same house?" Miss Comfort asked, pulling him from his musings.

"Doc Waller and Doc Drake? Sure. The house belongs to Doc and Grandma Waller, but Elsie, their niece, came to live with 'em 'bout the same time Bowen Drake showed up, and they fell in love and got married. Doc Drake studied science, medicine and all that stuff at some fancy college back East, so he joined Doc Waller in his practice. They all get along fine, and they added onto the house years ago, so there's plenty of room."

"Is there a lot of that around here?" she asked. "People moving in with family?"

"There's some—sometimes it's just easier than buildin' another house. Isn't there where you come from?"

"Yes, I suppose." She had a faraway look in her eye.

"How many folks in yer family?"

"My father and my six brothers."

"I only have my sister Emeline and my brother Tom. Ma and Pa moved to Oregon City a few years back on account of Pa feelin' poorly—they moved in with my aunt there."

"Do you see them often?"

"We see 'em when we can. I 'spect they'll come back to Clear Creek in the next few years—probably move in with myself or Emeline. Tom bein' sheriff and all, they might not wanna burden him." He glanced at her to gauge her reaction. "Ya wouldn't mind if they lived with us, would ya?"

She swallowed hard. "They're your family. How could I say no?"

"No more'n I could, I guess. If ya wanted yer pa to come live with us one day, I'd say yes."

He swore she cringed at his words. "I don't think we'll have to worry about that, Mr. Turner. I doubt my father would ever leave Georgia. Even if he did, he probably wouldn't come any closer than Denver."

"Why Denver?"

"I have an aunt there, my mother's sister. If something was to happen and he needed a place to go, he'd go there."

"Ya sound awful sure. How do ya know what yer Pa'll do?"

"I did live with him almost my entire life."

Good point. "What 'bout all those brothers of yers? Any of 'em hitched?"

"Not a one."

He stopped and looked at her. "Why not? They're all of age, right?"

Her look was forlorn. "I suppose…well…none of them have ever found the right girl."

"Too bad they cain't be mail-order husbands," he

said with a smile. "I can think of a few places to send 'em to find a wife."

"Mail-order husbands? Don't be ridiculous, Mr. Turner—there's no such thing."

"I know. But maybe it's 'bout time there was." He started walking again, and pointed to his left. "This here's the bank—Levi Stone works there. He and his wife Fina are our neighbors."

"Yes, that's been well-established," she said with a tiny smile. "And Mr. and Mrs. Adams are our other neighbors."

"Yep. Chase Adams is the blacksmith in town and runs the livery stable—did ya know that yet?"

"No, but I do now." She stopped and stared up the street. "I declare, but that is a lovely hotel."

Eli followed her gaze. "Yep, Mr. Van Cleet built it and spared no expense. Ya wanna see the inside?"

"Can we?" she asked, glancing over her shoulder at the mercantile. "Is there time?"

"'Course there is. In fact, it's almost teatime if'n my guess is right."

"Teatime?" she said, surprised.

"Sure—lotsa folks go to the hotel for afternoon tea." By now they'd reached Mulligan's Saloon, and he pointed at it. "Even Mr. Mulligan likes to go over and tip back a cup."

She smiled again, broader this time. "You're serious."

"'Course I am. Don't tell me ya don't believe me."

"I didn't say that," she said firmly. "Don't put words in my mouth, Mr. Turner."

Hmmm…for some reason that got her riled.

"I wasn't tryin' to. Come on, I'll show ya." They

started off again, and within moments were walking through the front doors of the hotel and into its lobby.

"Oh my," she said.

"Purty impressive, ain't it?"

She nodded and motioned him closer. "That's a rather large fellow behind the counter. He doesn't look anything like a hotel clerk."

"Lorcan? He used to be a fighter, 'til he lost his sight. He managed his parents' bookshop in Oregon City until Mr. Van Cleet came along and offered him this job. He got so good at it that Seth and Eloise Jones left to work on Seth's brother's ranch."

"I believe I heard something to that effect from Sadie."

"Won't take ya long to learn 'bout everyone in town—where they've been, what they've done. Everyone knows everyone's business 'round here."

She opened her mouth to comment, but never got a chance. "Hello, Eli," the hotel clerk said with an Irish brogue, though not as heavy as Mr. Mulligan's. "Here for tea?"

"Sure am, Lorcan—and I brought my future bride with me."

Lorcan stood, and Eli caught the way Miss Comfort's eyes widened as she noted him. "Mrs. Upton has everything ready as usual. Ada's in the dining room, and I'm sure she'd love to meet her. As would I, for that matter."

"Sure thing," Eli led her to the counter. "Lorcan Brody, meet Miss Pleasant Comfort."

"How do you do, Miss Comfort?" he asked, extending a huge, scarred hand.

Eli watched as she stared at Lorcan a moment. She'd

probably just noticed he really was blind. "Very well, thank you."

"She sounds nice," Lorcan said, smiling at Eli.

"She's right purty, I can tell ya that," Eli said with pride. Miss Comfort's cheeks turned crimson, which made his stomach feel funny inside. He liked it when she blushed. "We'll just mosey into the dinin' room now. Ya'll join us later, won't ya?"

"I'm waiting for Mr. Van Cleet, but I'll join you as soon as he and I are done."

"All right," Eli said. "In the meantime I'll introduce Miss Comfort here to Ada."

"You do that," Lorcan said and retook his seat.

Eli escorted Pleasant into the hotel dining room where at least a half a dozen tables had been set for tea. "How long has Mr. Brody been blind?" she asked him softly.

"Some six years, I think. He and his wife moved here about five years back, and it wasn't long before that he'd lost his sight fightin'. Seth Jones taught him everything he knew about the hotel and how to run it. I think that's why Mr. Van Cleet asked Lorcan to come in the first place. Seth wanted to help his brother run his ranch, and they knew someone'd hafta manage the hotel after he left."

"My my. For such a small town, there certainly is a lot going on here."

"That's because ya know the folks involved. When ya know everyone in town, ya know everythin' that's goin' on. In some big city, ya wouldn't think twice about a different hotel clerk greetin' ya when ya walked in. But when there's only one hotel, and one clerk…"

"I see what you mean."

"Eli Turner," a woman with a gentle Southern accent declared. That definitely got Miss Comfort's attention. She looked the woman up and down as she continued to talk. "Where have you been? We've not seen you at tea in ages."

"Howdy, Ada. I brought my future bride with me." He motioned to his intended. "Ada, meet Miss Pleasant Comfort."

"Hello, Miss Comfort. How are you liking Clear Creek?"

Miss Comfort stared at her a moment, as if expecting Ada to have said something else. "I'm afraid I'm still getting used to it. It's such a small town."

"Oh, you're from the South too," Ada stated. "I'm from New Orleans myself. And you?"

A tiny smile formed on Miss Comfort's lips. She had a lovely smile. Eli tried not to sigh in contentment. "Savannah, Georgia."

"Well then, you'll have to tell me what's been happening on that side of the country. It's been so long since I've been there."

Miss Comfort gave Ada a warm smile. "I'd love to."

Eli smiled to himself. He'd forgotten that Ada Brody was from Louisiana. At least now he knew his future bride would have one friend with whom she'd have something in common. He wanted her to have friends, wanted her to feel welcome in Clear Creek. Consarnit, he wanted to see her happy—so much so he could feel it in his gut. Now why did you suppose that was?

With a shake of his head he pulled a chair out for Pleasant, seated her, then did the same for Ada. He sat himself and listened to the two women get to know one another. Much to his surprise, he found he liked it.

* * *

"I was a mail-order bride too," Ada Brody said with a faraway look in her eye. "I remember the first time I saw Lorcan—he came flying out of a saloon window and landed in the street!"

Pleasant gasped. "He did what?!"

"Yes, I'd just gotten off the stage. His mother was there and was *furious*!"

Pleasant studied Ada Brody more closely. She was a pretty blonde and though her Southern accent was laced with Louisiana Creole, she had the bearing of a woman who'd been gently bred and raised. But she also had the gumption Pleasant recognized from working with Sadie, Belle, Honoria and especially Grandma Waller. These women had learned to deal with life out West and had become better for it. She hoped and prayed she could do the same in time.

She glanced at Eli, who sipped his tea as any gentleman would. He may not have been born and raised on a plantation, but that didn't mean he was without manners. So he didn't speak as eloquently as her father or brothers (thankfully, he didn't bellow like them either!), but that didn't mean he was any less a man.

"I'm sure you'll find Clear Creek to be very quaint and charming once you get used to it," Ada went on. "It is a little different here, I'll grant, but I've grown to love the town and everyone in it. So has Lorcan."

Speaking of Lorcan… "Hello, ladies, Eli," he said as he walked straight to their table unaided. Pleasant wondered how he managed to do it, then noticed a wiry older man behind Mr. Brody. Maybe he'd guided him into the dining room. "Might I join you?"

"Of course," Ada told him. "And, Miss Comfort, this

is Mr. Cyrus Van Cleet, owner of the hotel. Cyrus, this is Miss Pleasant Comfort."

"Happy to meet you, Miss Comfort," Mr. Van Cleet said. "Eli here has told me all about you."

Pleasant looked at her intended. "He has?"

"Of course. I often stop in at the sheriff's office when I'm in town to say hello to our boys. They protect the lot of us, you know—we should thank them every day."

"Oh yes, I…suppose so," she stammered. Back home she hadn't thought twice about such a thing.

The two men sat. "I hope my wife has been keeping you entertained, lass," Lorcan said with a smile. "But be wary. She's a talker."

"I am not!" Ada protested, glaring at him.

"Yes, you are. And don't look at me like that."

Pleasant, her mouth opening and closing like a guppy's, gaped at them. "How can he…"

"Know what sort of look I'm giving him?" Ada asked. "Marriage. It'll do that to you."

"I don't understand," Pleasant confessed.

"We've been through a lot, Lorcan and I," Ada said.

"Aye, that we have," he agreed.

"We know each other so well, he can tell what I might be doing without saying a word and vice-versa."

Pleasant glanced at Eli. Would they share such closeness? "What a wonderful thing."

Ada wrapped an arm through her husband's. "It certainly is."

"Do you have any children?" Pleasant asked, curious.

"Yes, a daughter," Ada said. "She's napping, but she should wake soon."

"Aye, and then there'll be no peace in the place," Lorcan said with a laugh.

"How old is she?"

"Five," Ada replied. "Going on twenty."

Now Eli laughed. "That's a good description of Aideen."

"Excuse me?" Pleasant said, not quite catching the name.

"Ay-*deen*," he pronounced. "It's an Irish name—ain't that right, Lorcan?"

"Aye, as Irish as they come. She definitely has a mind of her own, Miss Comfort. And isn't the wee bit embarrassed to let everyone know it."

"A willful child?"

"Not at all," Ada said. "We like to think of her as… independent."

"She's a smart little thing too," Mr. Van Cleet added.

"I hope to have me some smart younguns," Eli said.

Pleasant glanced at him and noted how the tips of his ears had gone pink. She tried to hide a smile but couldn't quite manage it.

"What's so funny?" he asked.

"Nothing at all," she assured him as heat crept into her cheeks. If she wasn't careful, they'd match Eli's ears.

"Uh-huh," he said in disbelief.

"Is someone blushing?" Lorcan asked.

Pleasant's head jerked in his direction. "How did you know?"

"Yes, how did you know Deputy Turner's ears are pink as rosebuds?" Mr. Van Cleet said teasingly.

"Cyrus!" Eli said as if scandalized.

Pleasant looked around the table. Everyone was smiling, sharing in Mr. Van Cleet's teasing. She relaxed and sighed. "Your ears *are* pink."

"I know. They always do that when I don't want them to."

Pleasant put a hand to her chest and giggled as more people came into the dining room for tea.

"You think it's funny my ears give me away?" he asked.

"I think it's rather adorable," she said.

His ears went crimson. "Oh great—there they go again!"

"How can you tell?" she asked, still giggling.

"On account they feel like they're on fire!"

"Somebody get this man a bucket of water!" Mr. Van Cleet called out.

"Cyrus, please…" Eli begged before he started laughing himself.

Pleasant could hold back no longer. She laughed out loud, vaguely aware of Eli smiling as the others smiled as well. Pretty soon the whole table had joined her.

Then the unthinkable: "So," Eli said through his chuckles, "ya wanna get hitched tomorrow?"

Chapter Twelve

"Tomorrow?!" Pleasant croaked, and quickly cleared her throat. "I mean, we can't."

"Why not?" Eli asked innocently.

Pleasant studied him, the brightness in his eyes. Merciful heavens, was he actually becoming enamored with her already? Not that that was a bad thing—what bride didn't want her future husband falling in love with her before they marry? But the thought of marriage itself frightened her. It would be so…final.

"Miss Comfort?"

"I…that is…my dress isn't finished! In fact, it's barely begun. Mrs….oh, what is her name? The preacher's wife. She and some of the ladies are meeting tomorrow at the church to work on it. You heard her say so yourself." She sounded panicked, probably because she was. She really needed to calm down.

Eli smiled gently as a woman arrived at the table and began pouring tea. "Yer afraid."

Pleasant could feel her lower lip vibrating like a violin string. "I am not afraid—d-d-don't be silly!"

The newcomer studied her. She was of a generous

build with curly blonde hair heavily streaked with grey, bright blue eyes and a very happy countenance. "This must be your bride, Eli."

"Sure is, Sally," he said.

Pleasant scanned the faces around the table—all of them staring at her.

"Don't worry, honey," Sally said. "Every bride's shaking in her skirts before she gets hitched, especially mail-order brides. But let me tell you, there isn't a finer eligible man around these parts than Eli. You'd do best to snatch him up quick."

Pleasant couldn't help but smile. "I'm glad you think so highly of him."

The woman stuck out a hand to her. "Sally Upton. And you are?"

She swallowed hard. "Pleasant Comfort."

Sally's eyes widened and she stifled a giggle. "Pleased to meet you." She turned to Eli. "Now don't rush the poor child. Let her have her dress—every bride feels prettier in a real wedding dress. Getting married in some calico number makes it not seem so real."

Eli glanced around the table. "Is that true?"

Ada smiled. "Oh, quite true. It's much nicer to be married in a dress made for the occasion."

He looked at Pleasant. "Then I guess I'll hafta wait."

She sighed in relief.

"Ya okay?" he asked.

"Yes, I'm fine, Mr. Turner."

"And that's another thing," Sally interjected with a giggle. "Why are you two being so formal? You're getting hitched, aren't you? You should be addressing each other by your Christian names. What's a few days between lovers?"

"Lovers!" Pleasant gasped.

"She means acquaintances," Ada said quickly.

"No, I don't," Sally insisted. "In a few days they're gonna be…"

"Very good friends!" Ada said, a little flustered. Lorcan almost choked, while Mr. Van Cleet shook with silent laughter as he studied the ceiling.

"Why don't we start with friends?" Eli suggested. "Call me Eli, like we talked about the other night."

Pleasant noticed her breathing was erratic. What was the matter with her? It wasn't as if they were going to marry that very minute. And even if they were, would that really be so bad?

She fidgeted in her chair. "Eli," she echoed.

"Pleasant" came out a whisper, the adoration in his eyes hard to miss. She noted again how handsome he was. Everyone spoke highly of him, and he'd shown her nothing but kindness since her arrival. What woman wouldn't want to marry a man like that? Yet she felt so afraid…

"There, that's better," Sally said. "You two should have been on a first-name basis from the beginning in my book."

"Now that that's settled," said Mr. Van Cleet, "why don't you serve the rest of the tea?"

"Oh! Yes, of course, Cyrus—coming right up!" Sally hurried over to a cart with plates of cookies, cakes and pies.

Pleasant took a deep breath and let it out slowly. Part of her wanted to bolt from the hotel and run out onto the prairie. If she felt like this marrying Mr. Turner—correction, *Eli*—then what would it have been like being forced to marry Rupert Jerney?

"Sally's right in that we don't stand too much on ceremony around here," Mr. Van Cleet said. "You can call me Cyrus if you want. I can't wait to introduce you to my wife Polly."

Pleasant smiled. "I look forward to meeting her." She studied the dining room—tables were filling up fast. "Does the whole town come here for tea?"

"Just 'bout," Eli said. "It's what ya might call a tradition."

Pleasant noted the newcomers were all glancing her way. "I recognize a few of them."

"Ya see Lena and Fina over there?" Eli pointed. "That's their husbands they're sittin' with. I'll introduce ya later. Might as well meet the neighbors."

She nodded, surprised that Mr. Adams, a blacksmith, would take time out for afternoon tea. Clear Creek, it seemed, had its own sort of civilization.

"We make more money from teatime than from guests staying at the hotel," Cyrus laughed. "But more and more folks stay here every year."

"Really?" Pleasant asked. "How many did you have last year?"

"Twelve," Lorcan said proudly.

Pleasant's eyes fluttered. Twelve?! Merciful heavens, what a reminder that she was in the back of the beyond! Her pampered life in big, bustling Savannah flashed before her eyes. This was another world, and in many ways a much smaller one. Maybe that's why she feared marrying Eli Turner—it wasn't so much *him* as *here*.

"Are you all right?" he asked, concerned.

She stared at him as tears stung her eyes. She'd made her choice; she would have to live with it. And though Clear Creek was small and isolated, the people were friendly (mostly) and Eli was nice. Besides, truffles could be found a few days away—make that a week or more, but still…

"Yes, I'm fine." Deep down, though, she knew she wasn't—yet.

After tea, they rode out to Eli's place. Pleasant felt a shiver of excitement at the thought. She would finally see where she was going to live! She hoped she hadn't ruined things by trying for the past few days to picture what the house looked like. After all, Eli Turner wasn't going to have a ranch house like the ones at the Triple-C. But she was excited all the same.

Eli rode his horse alongside the Cookes' wagon and made comments about Sally Upton's cookies, cakes and pies. Pleasant made a mental note to ask Sadie and Belle if they had any of her recipes. Eli obviously liked the woman's cooking, and she wanted to learn to make all the things he liked. She was determined to be a good wife, even if it did mean days of drudgery now and then. After all, one didn't have to do laundry every day.

"Well, this is it." Eli brought his horse to a halt, and Colin did the same with his team. Pleasant suddenly noticed that everyone was looking at her. She shrugged, unsure of what they wanted.

"Aren't you going to look?" Sadie asked.

Pleasant was so busy watching everyone else watch her that she hadn't noticed the little cabin on the other side of some trees. Merciful heavens, was that it? Maybe it was just a large chicken coop or something. "Um… where is it?" she asked hesitantly.

"Right through them trees." Eli kicked his horse forward.

Pleasant made a show of craning her neck to see.

Lord have mercy, but that had to be it. There were no other buildings other than a loafing shed. The man didn't even have a barn! She looked at him atop his horse, at the animal's small shelter, then spotted an even smaller structure with hay piled in it. "Heaven help me," she muttered.

"I know it ain't much," Eli said. "But it's roomy enough inside for two."

Pleasant nodded numbly. She was speechless, which was a good thing—she was afraid of what she might've said. It was exactly the one-room cabin everyone had promised. And she'd have to make the best of it. This was the life she'd chosen over one of loveless luxury with Rupert. "I...can't wait to see the inside," she said with a forced smile.

Eli dismounted as Colin brought the wagon to a stop again, set the brake and hopped down. "I must say, Eli, I can't wait to see what you've done with the place."

Eli dismounted, tied his horse to a hitching post in front of the tiny house, then grinned. "Well, I did have help."

"Help?" Pleasant said.

"His sister Emeline," Belle explained. "You know how bachelors are."

"No, I'm afraid I don't," she admitted.

"Oh, that's right," Belle said. "You and your brothers had servants. Around here, bachelors do what they can to clean up after themselves and cook, but...well, with no one around to see it, they can get a little slack. Hopefully Emeline has pulled the slack out of Eli's home."

Harrison and Colin helped the women down, then headed for the house. Eli was already at the front door and had it wide open, a welcoming smile on his face.

"After you, ladies." Colin swept a hand toward the entrance. Belle and Sadie entered, smiles on their faces.

Pleasant's expression was more one of trepidation as she slowly entered the humble dwelling. But though humble on the outside, the inside was something else entirely. "Oh my," she whispered. "How charming!"

"I hafta admit, my sister does know how to decorate," Eli said. "It didn't look nothin' like this a month ago. Your job'll be to keep it nice. Lord knows I try and I fail."

"Rather a hard task when all you do is eat and sleep here, old chap," Harrison said. "And sometimes have barely the time for that."

"You should've seen the original ranch house my brothers and I were raised in," Colin added. "It wasn't much more than this." He glanced upward. "The roof is good?"

"'Course," Eli told him. "Levi and I worked on it. Been through a few good rains already and ain't leaked one bit."

Pleasant's eyes drifted to the ceiling as well. "Oh dear—a leak would be bad, wouldn't it?" She glanced around at the sparse furnishings. There was a beautiful tablecloth on the small kitchen table tucked into one corner, near a brightly painted hutch, a little worktable and a cook stove. The opposite side of the cabin had a fireplace, a sofa, a rocking chair and a cozy rug between the sofa and fireplace. A trunk stood against the wall on one side of the fireplace, a small bookcase full of books on the other.

But it was the curtains that really gave the place charm—blue-and-white gingham trimmed with matching ruffles, very frilly for a bachelor like Eli but perfect for Pleasant and her tastes. She also noticed teacups hanging under a shelf on the wall near the table, with a matching teapot and saucers on top.

His sister obviously had good taste and had done everything she could with the space allowed. It was hard to imagine Eli being responsible for all the delicate feminine touches. Pleasant would have to thank his sister later.

"Well?" Eli said. "What do ya think?"

"It's small, but very charming." Pleasant glanced around again and notice a bed tucked into the back corner of the room. "Oh my. We don't have a separate bedroom?"

"Not yet. I ain't got 'round to buildin' us an upstairs."

Pleasant looked up again. "Upstairs? How does one get upstairs?"

Eli walked over to the bed and pointed at the ceiling. "There ain't no staircase yet, but there will be. Don't worry, there's enough room in the attic for a bedroom. I'm sure Levi'll help—he's real handy with things like that."

"I would imagine Chase is too," Belle said.

"Couldn't ask for better neighbors," Eli agreed with a smile. "I never woulda had this place up as quick as I did without their help."

Pleasant let her eyes wander around the room some more. It was a far cry from the huge plantation house at Comfort Fields. But then…she closed her eyes and reminded herself of the life of misery she'd escaped from. Better to be in a one-room shack with a kind man than have all the luxuries in the world with an awful one. Now if she could just keep remembering that, she'd be fine.

"There's a smokehouse out back, and a root cellar too," Eli said proudly. "Would ya like to see 'em?"

Smokehouse? Root cellar? Good heavens, Pleasant had never seen either type of structure in her life. "Certainly," she said, figuring that she'd better know where everything was.

Eli smiled and motioned the group toward the front door. "Follow me, everybody."

They went outside and walked around the house to the back. There was a small outbuilding Pleasant hadn't noticed before, having been hidden from the road. "Which one is that?" she asked.

"That's the smokehouse. I don't have nothin' in it yet, but I will." He pointed to his left. "I thought we might put a pigpen over there…"

"Pigs?" she squeaked. She didn't care for the beasts unless they were cured, baked and served on a platter. "You want to keep pigs?"

"Sure, why not?" he asked with a happy smile.

She studied her surroundings, and noticed there were no animals on the place other than his horse. "You have no livestock? No chickens? Nothing?" Good. She hoped it stayed that way. Especially when it came to pigs—yikes!

"No, I was waiting for ya to come along before I got any. That way ya can take care of 'em!"

Pleasant's eyes widened. "But I… I've never taken care of an animal in my life. Not even a puppy."

"No time like the present to start," Sadie said with a happy smile and a pat on the back. "Don't worry, taking care of animals is much easier than you might think. Certainly easier than taking care of a husband."

"I say, wife, that's not very fair," Harrison objected. "We are *not* hard to care for."

"So *you* say," Belle retorted with a wry smile.

Colin placed his fists on his hips. "You mean, after all the years we've been married, you're just *now* saying that I'm difficult?"

"I can vouch I'm nothing of the kind," Harrison glared at Sadie.

"I didn't say you were that difficult," Sadie shot back. "Only that you weren't as easy to care for as, say, a laying hen. Some days I wish I only had to scatter corn on the ground and leave you to it."

"Oh," Harrison replied. "Well, that's all right, then."

"Don't let 'em scare ya none, sweetie," Eli said with a grin, taking Pleasant by the hand. "I'm real easy to take care of. Just feed me a few meals every day, keep the house clean, maybe mend my clothes and I'm a happy man."

Harrison and Colin tried to hide smiles but failed miserably. "What are you two grinning about?" Pleasant asked, worry in her voice.

"Nothing to concern you, Miss Comfort," Harrison said. "You're going to marry a good man and have this lovely little cottage. It will be wonderful once Eli gets it done."

Pleasant's eyes brightened. *Cottage* did sound nicer than *shack*. It was all a matter of perspective, she supposed. "Well, so long as I don't have to climb a ladder to get to bed, I'll be fine."

"That's the spirit," Belle said with a smile. "And don't fret—Sadie and I will help too."

"Yes," Harrison agreed. "And we'll start things off by giving you a few cattle as a wedding present."

"Aw shucks, Harrison," Eli said. "Ya don't hafta do that."

"Perhaps, but we're happy to," Colin remarked.

Eli unexpectedly pulled Pleasant into his arms. "Ain't that wonderful? They're gonna give us some cows! I can't wait to teach ya how to milk one."

Pleasant paled. "I can hardly wait."

"If we don't get back to town and get our business done, you'll be waiting longer than you need to," Sadie said. "It's time we headed home."

Eli stared at Pleasant as if he just realized she was in his arms. Pleasant, on the other hand, was still thinking about cows and didn't really notice. "I guess I can wait a few more days," he said softly as he studied her. "But I don't think I can last much longer."

Pleasant blinked a few times as his words registered. "My dress," she said, reminding him in a voice just as soft. "We need to finish it."

"I know. I cain't wait to see ya in it. Yer gonna be the prettiest bride Clear Creek's ever seen."

She blushed. "I don't know about the prettiest, but... I do want to look nice for you. Every bride should look nice for her future husband on her wedding day."

"I agree." He smiled, let her go, wrapped her arm around his and escorted her to the wagon as the others trailed behind.

"Would you like to come join us for supper tomorrow, Eli?" Harrison asked.

"Don't mind if I do," he said, never taking his eyes from Pleasant's. His head suddenly spun to the other two men. "That is, if'n I don't have guard duty. If'n I do, I'll try to get word out to the ranch."

"No need—I'm sure one of us will be coming into town tomorrow," said Colin.

"We most certainly will," Sadie added. "We have Pleasant's dress to work on, remember?"

"There's your answer, Eli," Harrison said. "One way or another, we'll see you tomorrow."

Eli nodded, took Pleasant's hands in his and gave them a squeeze. "'Til tomorrow, then, sweetie. Ya have a nice rest of the afternoon and evenin', ya hear?"

Heat crept into her cheeks—and a few other places—and she took a deep breath as she stared at him. "I'll certainly try."

"Ya do that." He released her and helped her into the wagon as Harrison and Colin did the same with Sadie and Belle. With a slap of the lines Colin got the horses moving as everyone waved their goodbyes.

Pleasant's eyes lingered on Eli as they pulled away, and she took one last look at the tiny cottage—*keep calling it that, it helps*—that would be her home. Once again she reminded herself that becoming a mail-order bride had been the right thing to do. After all, she could've done a lot worse than Eli Turner.

Chapter Thirteen

The ladies' sewing circle went to work on Pleasant's dress the next day with a will. Were they anxious to see her wed? She had no idea, but she liked that they were trying to speed things along.

Yet when she thought of Eli's small cabin—*cottage, cottage...*—in comparison with the house at Comfort Fields, she cringed. She'd had servants, beautiful gowns, a bevy of brothers for protection (and, admittedly, a source of irritation) and a father who, until he ran out of money, doted on her.

She sighed as she tried her best to stitch. What did she miss most, her family or the money? Of course she missed her brothers, especially her twin Matt. They'd been very close growing up, but the war and the chaotic aftermath had driven a wedge between them, one that grew as the years passed. As the family's money dwindled, so did their relationship.

But she had to admit that Matt was growing into a fine young man. He had other interests—women and horses, for instance—and spent more and more time with his brothers. What did she expect him to do, sit around and discuss her latest new dress? Matt was grown up and that was that.

She did wonder how mad he was at her leaving the way she had. But she hadn't heard a peep out of any of them, and likely never would. They had no idea where she'd gone, and no way of finding out except maybe to wheedle it out of Aunt Phidelia. By the time they did, if they did, she'd be married. There'd be nothing they could do.

The morning wore on, and the ladies made good progress. They were just finishing up for the day when Pastor Josiah King, Annie's husband, came out of the church office to check on them. "How are things coming?"

"Very well," Annie said. "Eli and Miss Comfort could marry after church on Sunday if they wanted."

Preacher Jo, as he was called, smiled and looked at Pleasant. "My, my, that would be something."

Pleasant looked between him and his wife. "Sunday after church is fine with me. I'm sure Mr. Tur…er, Eli will think so too."

Preacher Jo laughed. "Oh, I know the two of you won't mind, and neither will the rest of the town. If we have the wedding Sunday after service, they'll all want to attend."

Pleasant blanched. "They will?! But…but they don't know me."

"They know Eli," he said. "Besides, we love weddings around here and the entire town has been to… oh, let me think, just about every one. Isn't that right, Annie?"

"I wasn't here for the first few," she commented. "And I don't know if you can count the one in the livery stable."

"Oh yes," he said with a chuckle. "We won't count that one."

The other ladies still present giggled. Pleasant glanced around the sewing circle, trying to figure out what the joke was. "You officiated a wedding in the livery stable?" she finally asked.

"Yes, though it was rather…unofficial."

Pleasant's face screwed up in disgust. "Who in their right mind wants to get married in a livery stable?"

Preacher Jo's smile was tight-lipped. "No one. Including, in that case, the bride and groom. Though they did come around."

"He's talking about Mr. Berg, our old blacksmith at the time, and Madeline Van Zuyen," Belle muttered. "You've heard us mention them before."

"Yes, but why would they get married in the livery?"

"It was a shotgun wedding," Grandma Waller clarified. "With actual shotguns."

Pleasant's mouth flopped open. "Wha-a-a-at?!"

Preacher Jo nodded to himself in recollection. "Let's see, that was back in '59. The third wedding I ever performed here—and still the only one where I had to threaten to take an English duke's gun away."

"And shove it up his nose," Grandma added.

Pleasant's head was spinning. She'd heard of shotgun weddings, but this was the first time she'd met someone involved in one, let alone one so bizarre. "Oh, that poor girl."

"Not hardly," Preacher Jo said. "Though Mr. Berg did get more than he bargained for when he got hitched to Madeline Van Zuyen, that's for sure."

The ladies laughed in agreement, and Pleasant knew she was missing something. Had Belle or Sadie mentioned anything out of the ordinary about the couple? Not that she recalled, but they'd spoken only briefly of them…

"Has anyone heard from them lately?" Mary Mulligan asked.

"Not for a while now," Sadie said. "But I imagine we'll get a letter soon."

Pleasant shook herself. Enough of this—she needed to concentrate on her wedding. "I suppose I don't mind the town attending my wedding if Eli doesn't." Truth be told, she'd always dreamed of a big wedding with a church full of people. It wouldn't be exactly what she'd pictured in her head—she'd hardly know most of the attendees—but that was a minor quibble. However… "Oh dear."

"What's the matter?" Sadie asked.

"If all those people stay after church just to watch us get married, what about cake?"

"Cake?" Preacher Jo laughed. "My dear Miss Comfort, we'll let Mrs. Upton and Mrs. Dunnigan take care of the wedding supper and cake. Don't you worry, they'll have it well in hand."

"Wedding supper?" Pleasant said, a half-smile on her face.

"Of course," said Grandma. "You've got to have a wedding supper at the hotel after the ceremony. Everyone pitches in and brings something. There'll be plenty of food."

Pleasant put a hand to her chest and smiled, tears in her eyes. She'd never dreamed she'd be in the midst of so many kind people. "You'd do that for Eli and me?"

"Naturally," Grandma said. "I told you before—

around here we help each other. You'd better get used to it."

Pleasant covered her mouth with a hand to stifle a sob. She didn't know why she was getting so emotional all of a sudden. Maybe because these near-strangers were so willing to help her and wanted to see that she and Eli were happy. Speaking of Eli, she couldn't wait to tell him!

Yes, there was something far more important than the money she'd grown up with. The people of Clear Creek genuinely cared about one another. Their love and respect wasn't hidden away deep within their own family, never to be seen beyond the borders of their property. No, they shared it freely, even with a stranger in their midst. "Thank you...so much. I think Sunday is a fine idea."

"It's settled, then!" Mary announced. "I'll let everyone else know to get cooking."

"I'll handle the decorations, as is my usual post," Sadie said.

"And we'll be sure the dress is done in time," chimed in Belle.

"I'll make some pies for Eli," Grandma volunteered. "In case he has a hard time waiting 'til Sunday."

Pleasant cocked her head in confusion. "Pies?"

Preacher Jo laughed. "Around here it's a tradition to, ah, keep a groom well-stocked with pies until he's married. To distract him from getting ahead of things."

Grandma nodded. "Otherwise he's apt to do something foolish before his wedding night."

Pleasant slowly began to understand, and a smile formed on her face. "Well, I declare, I suppose it's better than whiskey."

"Tastier too," Grandma said. "Besides, a man in his cups isn't worth his salt the next day."

"Though neither is a man with an upset stomach," Preacher Jo replied.

"Depends on how many pies there are," Belle said with a smile. "Okay, let's meet here again tomorrow, ladies. We have a wedding to plan!"

Pleasant sat, unable to hold back her tears. The folks back home, nice as they were, wouldn't dream of holding a wedding like this. They'd call it undignified, say that the people of Clear Creek were beneath them. She had thought that way, until she gave everything up and made a run for it. But now she saw that happiness far outweighed a bank account. And it wasn't as if marrying Eli Turner would cause her to starve—he would do his best to provide for and protect her.

"Now there's no need for tears, child." Grandma handed her a handkerchief.

"I'm sorry, it's just that…you've all been so very kind to me and I feel like I don't deserve it."

"What makes you say that?" Sadie asked. "Just because you're new in town doesn't mean we're going to treat you any different than anyone else. You're marrying Eli, our friend. Of course we're going to welcome you with open arms."

Pleasant sniffed back her tears and dabbed at her nose with the handkerchief. "Where I come from, things are much different."

"You and your kin must have suffered greatly with the war," Preacher Jo stated. "I imagine trust is a hard thing to come by."

She nodded. "Yes, very. You'd think things would be so much better by now, but there are still so many out to…well, never mind." She looked at the concerned faces staring back at her. "I'm glad I'm here."

Sadie smiled. "And we're glad to have you. Now let's get you home. Eli is coming to supper."

Pleasant helped take the biscuits out of the oven, picked up the platter of fried chicken Sadie had prepared and set it on the kitchen table. Jefferson, Edith and the Kincaids were having supper in their own homes this evening, so the family was eating in the kitchen.

"Won't Eli be surprised when he finds you baked this pie all by yourself?" Sadie asked.

"I just hope it turned out all right," she replied nervously. "It's my first real pie."

"Well, the first one without one of us hovering over you," Belle added with a smile. "I'm sure he'll love it. Come to think of it, where is Eli? He should be here by now."

"I hope he's able to make it," Pleasant said. "This pie actually looks good."

"You want to marry him, don't you?" Belle asked.

"What kind of a question is that?" Pleasant asked. "It's what I came here for."

"Yes, but there's getting married because you're a mail-order bride, and there's getting married because you want to, because you *like* Eli."

"Oh, that." Pleasant blushed. "Yes, I am beginning to like him a lot. I suppose that helps, as I'm to marry him on Sunday."

"I can't say it enough—he'll make you a wonderful husband," said Sadie.

"I'm beginning to see that," Pleasant admitted as she

hung her head. "Now I'm more concerned about being a wonderful wife."

"It'll come to you in time," Sadie assured. "It took Belle and me a while too, and I'm not talking about just cleaning, sewing, cooking and doing a man's laundry. You have to listen to him, encourage him, counsel him at times."

"Merciful heavens, are men really that helpless?" Pleasant asked in surprise.

"Not necessarily," Belle said. "But they do depend on us. And they need our respect and understanding most of all."

"What about us?" Pleasant asked. "What about our needs?"

"You have to be sure he knows what they are," Belle said. "If there's one thing I've learned from being married all these years, it's that they can't read our minds. After you've educated your husband, it's up to him to do what needs to be done."

"Just as it's up to you to see to his needs," Sadie added. "It takes two to make a marriage—it can't be one-sided. But Eli is perfectly capable, willing and, dare I say, eager to do his part."

Pleasant blew out a breath. "I hope I make a good wife. I hate to admit this, but I've never had to be responsible for anyone before. Not even myself, really."

"We know," Belle said. "We were the same before we got married."

"That's good to know." Pleasant hugged them both.

"You're going to be a wonderful wife," Belle said. "Stop fretting about it."

Pleasant pulled away and looked at them. "I know

I shouldn't worry so, but it's hard when it's something I've never done before."

A knock sounded at the front door, interrupting the conversation. "That must be Eli," Belle said. "Now pull yourself together and let's have a nice supper."

Pleasant nodded, took one last look at her beautiful pie, then went to finish setting the table.

Supper couldn't get over fast enough. Pleasant was eager to see what Eli thought of her apple pie. She'd used a recipe Grandma Waller had given Belle years ago and insisted neither Belle nor Sadie tell her what to do.

Making that pie made her realize she'd never put much effort into anything before. All she'd had to concern herself with in Savannah was looking good and having a good time. Her father had taken care of everything. She now saw how spoiled she'd been—so much so that she wasn't willing to face a marriage to Rupert Jerney to save her family's beloved home.

Guilt assailed her as she watched her intended wipe his mouth with a napkin. Could she have made things work with Rupert? Had she only been thinking of herself when she ran away? Well, there was no way of knowing now. She shut the thoughts out of her mind and concentrated on Eli. "Did you enjoy your meal?" she asked.

"Sure 'nough did, sweetie." He looked at Sadie. "I think ya make the best fried chicken in town, Sadie Cooke. Harrison's a lucky fella. And I'd consider myself lucky if'n ya gave Pleasant the recipe."

"I'll teach her how to make it myself," Sadie said.

"Much obliged." He grinned and winked at Pleasant. "Wouldn't do no good to teach me. Tom's always tellin' me how bad my coffee is. I cain't imagine what I'd do to fried chicken."

They all laughed at that. "Let's hope none of us have to find out," Harrison said. "Now how about dessert in the parlor? I hear *someone* made a delicious pie." Everyone's eyes fixed on Pleasant.

She felt herself blush and looked at the table. "I may have whipped one up," she said shyly.

"You made the pie again?" Eli asked.

"Without any help from us," Belle was quick to say. "She used one of Grandma's recipes."

"Really?" he said. "Which one?"

"Apple," Pleasant said with a smile. "I hope you like it."

"Like it? I'm sure I'll love it! Let's get to the parlor."

The men retired to the parlor as the women brought the pie and coffee. Pleasant hadn't felt this excited about something since her father gave her a pony when she was seven. Merciful heavens, who would've thought a pie would be as exciting as a pony? Once everyone was served, she sat on the settee next to Eli and tried not to fidget.

Eli watched her and grinned. "If'n this turns out just like Grandma Waller's, I'm gonna have to marry ya right now."

Pleasant gasped. "Because of a piece of pie?"

"No, 'cause of the big kiss I'll give ya! Trust me, it'll be downright scandalous."

Harrison's brow furrowed. "A peck of thanks on the cheek will do, Eli," he warned.

"Oh Papa, really," Honoria said.

"It's not proper for him to, as he says, kiss her scandalously before they marry," Harrison stated.

"Then I'll be sure to bake any future beau of mine pies in private," Honoria said with the tiniest hint of a smirk.

Harrison came out of his chair like a shot. "You'll do no such thing! That is not what pie is for!"

"So I've learned," Pleasant said. "You people should write a book on the subject."

The Cookes laughed. "It's being done," Colin said. "Our cousins Imogene and Cutty are seeing to it. It was bound to happen eventually. Who knows if it will ever be published?"

"It could," Sadie said.

Pleasant gasped. While they were talking, Eli had taken a bite. Everyone watched as he slowly chewed. "Don't tease me," she said. "And be honest!"

He swallowed. "Dagnabit!"

Pleasant's face twisted up with concern. "What's the matter with it? You didn't bite into an apple seed, did you?"

"*Dagnabit*...that's good!" He took another bite.

Pleasant's shoulders slumped in relief as she watched the others dig in. She'd passed Eli's test—that was the important part.

"I dare say, Miss Comfort," Colin said. "But if you're this nervous over a dessert, what are you going to be like when you give your first party?"

"Party?" she squeaked. Visions of dozens of people stuffed into Eli's tiny cabin flashed before her. "Why would I give a party?"

"That's a wonderful idea," Sadie said. "You should give a party for your new house!"

"Yes, you'll find folks around here do love a good party," Harrison added. "And will use any excuse to have one. There will be your wedding supper, of course, but a house party does sound like fun. I'm sure the two of you need a few things."

Pleasant went pale. "I've…never heard of…what do you mean, need a few things?"

"Because you've just married of course," Harrison said. "And the house *is* new."

"I declare, I've never heard of such a thing," she said more to herself than anyone else.

"Neither had we until Mrs. MacDonald—she's a friend of the family—told us about them," Colin explained. "Apparently they have them all the time where she comes from."

"Where does she come from?" Pleasant asked.

The Cookes looked at each other. "By Jove, none of us have ever thought to ask," Harrison said. "Back East someplace, I believe."

"Well, I think it's a lovely idea," Belle said. "After your wedding, we'll plan it."

"Hosting a party in that tiny…" Pleasant stopped and made a show of clearing her throat. "…in that cute little cottage?"

"Maybe we oughta wait until I get the attic bedroom done," Eli suggested. "Then we'd have more room for folks."

"Jolly good—we'll help!" Harrison volunteered. "Won't we, brother?"

"Of course," Colin said. "The sooner you get the job done, the sooner we can have the party. In fact, we'll rope Logan into it as well. Another pair of hands is always welcome."

"Shucks, fellas," Eli said. "Ya don't hafta do that. Chase and Levi should be enough."

"Consider it another wedding gift," Colin said. "Besides, it will take forever if you're the only three working on it. Each can only spare a day here and there."

Eli sighed. "True 'nough. I guess I cain't argue with that."

"Then it's all settled," Harrison said. "After your wedding on Sunday, we'll get to it."

Eli looked at Pleasant and winked. "Ain't it nice to have such great folks 'round?"

She smiled in contentment. "Indeed. It's like an answer to a prayer."

"Well then, welcome to Clear Creek, sweetie!" He leaned toward her, glanced at an unsuspecting Harrison—and kissed her right on the mouth!

"Eli!" Harrison cried and popped out of his chair.

"That's giving it to her, Eli!" Honoria called just as loudly.

Harrison's head snapped around to her as he gasped. "You keep quiet, young lady! That—" He pointed at the kissing couple. "—is *not* what pie is about!"

Honoria started to laugh. "Then why are you letting them, Papa?" she asked in delight.

Harrison gawked at the couple. "Eli Turner! Take your lips off of that woman!"

Eli broke the kiss. Pleasant sat breathless, able only to stare at him in bewilderment. Eli, however, looked delighted.

"Now, Harrison…" Sadie interjected, trying to calm him down.

"I think it's time Mr. Turner went home!" Harrison

exclaimed as he crossed to the settee, grabbed Eli's arm and yanked him to his feet.

Eli didn't care, his eyes intent on his future bride. "Like I said, sweetie, now I'm gonna have to marry ya tomorrow."

Pleasant stared at him in wonder and nodded.

Chapter Fourteen

That night Pleasant lay in her bed and stared at the ceiling, still in awe of the kiss Eli had bestowed upon her. Harrison was upset over it for hours after. Merciful heavens, if the man was like this with her, practically a stranger, what was he going to be like when Honoria was courting?

She sighed in resignation. "Poor girl," she muttered. Any beau of Honoria's would be lucky to survive long enough to wed!

She smiled as she turned over and snuggled beneath the covers. Thank Heaven Sadie had sent the children upstairs to play after supper, or they'd have witnessed Eli's ardor. The poor little dears would never look at pie the same again. *She* would never look at one the same again, that was certain. In fact, she wasn't sure what Harrison was more upset about: Eli's kiss, or that they'd given pie a whole new meaning in Clear Creek.

She was never going to get to sleep at this rate. So she thought of her wedding dress and what would take place over the next few days. Sunday couldn't come quick enough now. She couldn't understand how a single kiss could make her feel so…so…hmmm, how did she feel? Other than stupendously wonderful, of course!

Pleasant giggled and went back to staring at the ceiling, her eyes bright with anticipation. "I couldn't possibly be falling in love. Could I?" She supposed she could.

But what did it feel like to be in love? She had no idea. Maybe she should ask Sadie or Belle. That might be embarrassing…but she shouldn't be embarrassed asking friends about such things—and the two women were her friends now. Which of her friends back home would help her as much as these two women had so far?

It was a sobering thought, one that convinced her all the more that she'd made the right decision in becoming a mail-order bride. She would miss her family and Comfort Fields, but who knew how long it would take her brothers and father to come around to her way of thinking? She wouldn't miss Rupert Jerney at all—her life with him would have been beyond miserable. She just knew it.

Now that she better understood the fear holding her back from marrying Eli, it had dissipated considerably. Money wasn't everything, and she was quickly learning that good friends were much more important than material possessions. The people of Clear Creek had shown her that.

She breathed another sigh of contentment, closed her eyes and finally went to sleep.

The next day, the women went to town and joined the other ladies at the church to work on her dress. Unfortunately, she didn't see Eli that day. He got stuck with guard duty, a job that extended into the evening as Henry Fig had caught a cold. That meant she didn't see him the following day either—he was probably at home catching up on his sleep.

It didn't help when Fanny informed the other women that even though Henry was back to work and feeling better, he wanted to be home at night with her. That meant Eli was stuck on the night watch again. His brother, the sheriff, was out of town, checking on the outlying farms—there were reports of other outlaws slinking about, and he wanted to make sure folks were taking precautions.

At this rate, Pleasant would be lucky to see Eli before Sunday. At least she knew she'd see him then. It was their wedding day, after all.

"Don't worry, I'm sure you'll meet with your groom before the big day," Belle assured her as they entered the church on Friday.

"I hope so," she said. "I... I miss him."

"That's a good thing," Belle said. "And who knows, perhaps you'll see him today."

Pleasant smiled at the thought. She hadn't been able to stop thinking about his kiss since that fateful dessert. She'd been baking pies ever since (much to Harrison's dismay) and each one sent her into a dreamlike state as she thought about her future husband. What would his kiss be like on their wedding day? And what would Harrison Cooke do then? She giggled at the thought as she took a seat.

"What's so funny?" Sadie asked.

The giggle turned into a laugh. "Nothing, really. Just thinking."

"Well I'm glad to see you so happy," Sadie said. "Come Sunday everyone will be."

"Why is that?"

"Because we haven't had a wedding here in a long time. Though as our children grow, I suspect we'll see quite a few in the future."

Pleasant glanced at Honoria across the church, speaking with Annie. "Yes, I would imagine so."

Sadie caught her looking at her daughter. "Though the wedding after yours might take a while to come about. We do seem to have a shortage of acceptable men."

"Too old or too young?" Pleasant asked.

"Both. Thankfully Honoria doesn't seem to mind. Marriage doesn't much interest her yet. But it will."

"Of course it will. I became a mail-order bride because I had to—I wasn't interested in marriage yet either."

Sadie stiffened. "You *had* to?"

"Because of…economics, you see. There's no end of money trouble where I come from." It was a version of the truth.

"Ah, I understand," Sadie said with a nod. "Now while you and the rest of the ladies are finishing up your dress, I'll be at the hotel discussing the decorations with Ada and Sally."

Pleasant nodded as relief washed over her. She didn't want to tell them yet exactly why she'd left. She should, however, pen a quick note to Mrs. Pettigrew to let her know she'd arrived safely and that by the time the letter arrived, she'd be married.

Mary Mulligan came in, interrupting her thoughts. She, Annie, Belle, Sadie and Pleasant herself had done most of the fine stitch work the previous day. Fanny Fig and Irene Dunnigan had showed up, saw they weren't really needed and went back to their own business.

A good thing, as Pleasant learned more in a smaller group—and when the two most volatile members of the sewing circle weren't sniping at her or each other.

Anyway, the dress should be done today, which would leave them all free to work on the decorations tomorrow, and any cooking and baking that remained. Back home Pleasant wouldn't have had to lift a finger except to order everyone around. But doing the work herself made her feel more satisfied than she ever had in her life. The same was true with baking a pie or helping Sadie and Belle prepare meals. Merciful heavens, she even discovered she didn't mind ironing!

What would her friends back in Savannah think? Easy—she'd be a laughingstock. But if her father had lost Comfort Fields, they'd have been a laughingstock anyway. She might as well be on the other side of the country and happy.

She wondered how her brothers were doing, and if they'd forgiven her for running away. Would she ever see them again? If she did, would they be willing to speak to her? She might never know. It was a price she knew she might have to pay for leaving. But Eli was wonderful, as were the people of Clear Creek. If not for them, she might well be lost in despair at this point.

They finished the dress that afternoon, organized the decorations, went home, made dinner…and before Pleasant knew it, Saturday had arrived. The women spent the entire day cooking and baking, just as she'd anticipated, and by the time supper came around, she was exhausted.

"We were hoping Eli would join us for supper," Belle said. "But I think he's got guard duty again tonight."

"How much longer will the outlaws be in Clear Creek?" Pleasant asked.

"At least until the judge comes through, which I imagine will be soon. Perhaps even Monday."

"What a relief that will be," she said. "I would hate to be home by myself every night after we're married."

"Oh dear, that would be awful," Belle agreed with a giggle. "It wouldn't be much of a honeymoon without Eli. But I'm sure Sheriff Turner will work something out—he's back now."

"I hope he does," Pleasant said. "Otherwise I'll be a very lonely bride."

"We can't have that," Belle said with a wink.

Pleasant blushed. Over the last few days the Cooke women had taken it upon themselves to explain to her the finer points of the marriage bed. As it turned out, a lot more than kissing went on behind closed doors. Pleasant felt her blush deepen and turned her face away in order to hide it.

Thankfully Belle started talking again. "Aunt Irene's in an uproar over the wedding cake. She doesn't understand why she can't have a go at making one for once, and why she's always stuck with the supper."

"Has it become a tradition for Sally to make the cakes and your aunt to be in charge of the main meal?" Pleasant asked, glad for the change of subject.

"I guess you could say so. We've been doing it this way for so many years, no one thinks to change it."

"It's a little late for her to be arguing about it, isn't it?" Sadie argued.

"Maybe we should tell them that for the next wedding, they'll have to switch," Belle suggested.

"That's a great idea," Sadie said. "I'll pull them aside tomorrow at some point and tell them."

"I don't care who does what, I'm just glad everyone's so willing to do it," Pleasant said, her cheeks still pink. "I wasn't expecting anything from anyone. In fact, I thought I'd get off the stage and be married the same day."

"I'm sure you did," said Sadie. "But that doesn't happen very often around here. Sometimes, yes, but for the most part the men around here like to court their brides for a few days at least. Some of them, a few weeks."

"Which brides were more nervous?" Pleasant asked. "The ones that got married right away or the ones that waited?"

Sadie laughed. "It all depended on the circumstances. Each one was so different. We'll have to tell you about them all someday."

"Like the shotgun wedding in the livery stable?" Pleasant asked with a bemused look.

"Exactly," Sadie said. "That we'll have to do over tea—it might take a while. There was a lot more involved than the shotgun part."

The evening wore on, and still no Eli. He obviously wasn't going to join them, which meant Pleasant wouldn't see him until tomorrow. Oh well, wasn't it supposed to be bad luck for the groom to see his bride before the wedding anyway? Did the night before count?

After supper she helped Belle and Sadie do the dishes, then heated some water for a bath. She wanted to look her best tomorrow, and a hot bath and a chance to wash her hair would definitely help. Unfortunately, neither helped her sleep that night. Instead, Eli's incredible kiss over their plates of pie haunted her. She spent the time imagining another and another and still another, each kiss sweeter than the last.

By the time Pleasant did fall asleep, her last thought was that she would be baking a lot of pies.

"I'm so nervous!" Pleasant said as Mary, Annie and Belle helped her into her wedding dress in the church office. She'd stowed it there rather than wear it through Sunday service. Besides, she didn't want Eli to see it until she walked down the aisle. Provided he made it—she still hadn't seen him!

It had been all she could do to sit through the service. At the end, Preacher Jo announced they'd have a little break before the wedding began so folks could go outside to visit and stretch their legs or use the privy out back. Now the pews were re-filling fast.

"Ye wouldn't be a normal bride if ye weren't nervous," Mary remarked as she buttoned up the back of Pleasant's dress. "Now hold still so I can get all of these. Where's yer veil?"

"Merciful heavens!" Pleasant said, panicked. "None of us thought about a veil!"

"I did!" Irene shoved her way into the office. "Same thing happened with the last two brides that got married here!"

"Oh Auntie," Belle said. "What would we do without you?"

"A whole lot worse," Irene snapped. "I suppose it's a good thing I didn't have a lot of extra work at the mercantile. Otherwise I wouldn't have had time to sew this together."

"Thank you." Pleasant admired the veil in Mrs. Dunnigan's hands.

The grouchy woman's face softened. "Think nothing of it, dear. Now put it on and let's have a look at you."

Sadie helped Pleasant pin the veil to her hair, then stepped back to take in Irene's handiwork. "It's lovely."

"I wish there was a mirror in here," Pleasant said nervously. "Will Eli like it?"

"He'd better," Irene grumbled.

"Oh yes," Belle assured her. "He's going to bust a gut when he sees you."

"I declare, but that sounds so…disgusting."

"You've never heard that expression?" Sadie asked.

"No, I haven't. I suppose I've said quite a few things that you've never heard, though. Right now I can't think of a one of them, I'm too nervous."

The other women laughed. "Ye're beautiful, lass," Mary said. "Now I'd best get out there. Jefferson Cooke is waiting for ye to give ye away, Miss Comfort. Just use the office door that goes outside, walk around the building to the front and ye'll find him."

"Oh my heavens," Pleasant said in a rush and put a hand to her temple. "That's another thing I never thought about—giving the bride away."

"It's become Jefferson's regular duty with mail-order brides," Sadie said. "Doc Waller's done the job a few times too."

"They like to think of themselves as the fathers of Clear Creek," Belle added as they began to usher Pleasant toward the door. "If we'd been thinking, we'd have let Cyrus do the job. He is technically the mayor, after all."

"He can give away the next one," Sadie said as they exited the side door and into the bright sunshine.

Several townsfolk milling about took one look at

Pleasant and began to ooh and ahh over her dress. Sadie shooed them away, and they hurried to the front of the church to go back in and reclaim their seats. The women waited a few moments, then followed.

Pleasant's stomach flipped as her palms started to sweat. "I think I need some water," she gasped.

"Good heavens," Belle said. "You really are nervous."

"I can't help it—I feel like I'm about to step off a cliff."

Sadie and Belle stopped in front of the church and looked at her. "You *do* want to marry Eli, don't you?" Sadie asked.

"Of course I do! It's just that this makes everything so…" She swallowed hard. "…final."

"What do you mean by that?" Sadie asked, arching an eyebrow. "You aren't running from anything, are you, Pleasant?"

"No! I mean, I'm not running from the law if that's what you think. I may have left in a hurry, but—"

"Why did you leave in such a hurry?" Belle asked.

"It's a long story. Well, it's not, really…oh, never mind about all that. I'll be all right—just give me a moment."

Belle and Sadie exchanged a quick look before nodding in agreement. "We'll let Jefferson know you're ready," Sadie said, grabbed Belle by the hand and dragged her into the church.

Pleasant stood and took a few deep breaths to calm herself. This was it! She was about to be married! She shut her eyes tight against the tears that threatened. On the one hand, she was ecstatic to be marrying Eli. Over the last three days the Cooke family had regaled her with tales about her future husband, which helped make up for not getting to see him. The more she heard, the more she liked him.

And who wouldn't? He was kind, gentle, strong, handsome and considered a hero by many in town. People respected him and admired his character. He was indeed a good man, and she couldn't have made a better choice. Or rather, Mrs. Pettigrew couldn't have.

How had the woman known? Because on the other hand, the last sort of man Pleasant would've pictured herself with was a poor one. Yet here she was, marrying a simple deputy who lived in a one-room cab-*cottage* with a few frilly curtains. It was nowhere near what she was used to, yet at this point it represented a tiny slice of Heaven.

For the first time in her life, Pleasant would have peace and solitude, and a chance to get to know someone she had yet to meet—herself.

She looked back on the person she'd been at Comfort Fields, and realized she didn't like that little brat very much. She was spoiled, haughty and thought herself above the people around her, including many of her friends. Unfortunately, most of those friends thought the same thing about her and each other. What a bunch of snobs they were—and she the worst of the bunch. Though she hadn't realized it until recently.

"Thank you, Mrs. Pettigrew," she whispered to herself. "I'll have to write you another letter and tell you all about this." She lifted the skirt of her wedding dress and went up the church steps.

Chapter Fifteen

"Well, are ya ready, Missy?" Jefferson asked as he offered Pleasant his arm.

"I suppose so," she said, a tremor in her voice.

"Don't ya worry none—all brides are nervous," he said softly.

"I… I wish my family could…" Pleasant stopped. Did she, really?

"Of course ya do," Jefferson said. "What bride don't want her family at her weddin'? I wish they could be here too—love to meet them."

She wrapped her arm through his, glad she hadn't said any more about her family. To do so might only raise a lot of questions, and she'd have to tell them what she'd done. She wasn't ready to do that yet, or to think about writing her brothers and father to let them know she was all right and happily wed. She'd pen a letter to Mrs. Pettigrew before she did that. Before *that*, she wanted to get through the ceremony first.

The wedding march drifted through the open doors to where they stood. "That's our cue, Missy," Jefferson said with a smile. "Let's get ya married!"

Pleasant swallowed hard and focused her mind on her intended. She hadn't seen Eli for days, and hoped he liked what he saw when she walked down the aisle.

They entered the church and started the slow march. It was so dark after being out in the bright sunshine, and Pleasant had to squint to see Eli standing at the altar. The townspeople murmured about her dress as they passed, which bolstered her courage. If they liked how she looked, Eli certainly should.

When she reached the middle of the church she gasped. They stared at each other as she approached, and it was all she could do to keep from crying. He was resplendent in a dark grey evening suit with tails, a white shirt, pearl-gray tie and even a diamond tie pin! He must have borrowed all of that—it was the only explanation. No small-town lawman could afford such an extravagance. It had to belong to one of the Cooke brothers. They were the only ones she could think of in Clear Creek who would own such clothing.

Eli stood and waited as Jefferson guided her the last few steps. Jefferson stopped in front of Preacher Jo, a huge smile on his face, as the couple continued to gawk at each other. "Eli, you have a lovely bride," Preacher Jo commented in a low voice.

Eli swallowed hard, his Adam's apple bobbing, and squeaked, "I... I sure do."

Preacher Jo gazed at the couple, looking proud as a peacock. "What say I marry these two?" he called to the church.

A cheer went up. Pleasant jumped at the sound and looked over her shoulder. Sadie and Belle weren't kidding when they said the town loved weddings! She quickly locked eyes with Eli again.

"Ahem," Preacher Jo said, and the congregation quickly quieted. "Dearly beloved, we are gathered here today in the presence of God to join these two young people together in holy matrimony. Can I have an amen?"

"Amen!" the crowd called back with no shortage of smiles and laughter.

Pleasant's mouth dropped open. The people in the pews were genuinely having a good time. She smiled as she faced front again, thoroughly enthralled. She'd never see this sort of thing back in Savannah.

"Who gives this woman?" Preacher Jo inquired.

"Ya don't have to ask, Preacher Jo!" some wag called from the back of the church.

"Jefferson!" a few others yelled.

Preacher Jo did his best not to laugh, and failed. "Forgive me," he told Eli and Pleasant. "But as you can see, everyone is in an exceptionally good mood today."

"We see that," Eli commented with a chuckle.

"Anyway," Preacher Jo said, "now you all know that the bond and covenant of marriage was established by God in creation…"

Pleasant's stomach picked that moment to growl so loud that Eli flinched beside her.

Preacher Jo stopped, looked at her with his eyebrows raised, smiled and went on. "…and our Lord Jesus Christ adorned this manner of life by His presence and first miracle at the wedding in Cana of Galilee."

Her stomach growled even louder this time. She knew she should have eaten something earlier, but she'd been too nervous.

Preacher Jo put a fist to his mouth and made a show of clearing his throat. He continued with the ceremony, and Pleasant thanked the Lord above that no one had started laughing. She wasn't sure what she'd do if the preacher or Eli had, and she suspected the whole church would have exploded in hysterics. Merciful heavens, she'd be mortified! A small snort escaped her as she pictured the scene, and she quickly put a hand to her mouth.

"…therefore marriage is not to be entered into unadvisedly or lightly, but reverently, deliberately and in accordance with the purposes for which it was instituted by God." Preacher Jo arched an eyebrow at her. "Are you all right?"

Pleasant, much to her horror, was doing everything *she* could not to burst into laughter! And here she'd pictured the townspeople doing so. She glanced at Eli, who was also looking oddly at her. She waved a hand in front of her. "I'm fine, really," she managed. Maybe everything had suddenly caught up to her and she was going round the bend!

Preacher Jo took a deep breath and continued. "Well, ah…" A snort of laughter escaped him.

"Don't!" she pleaded, a hand to her chest. She then put it over her mouth and shut her eyes tight.

"Land sakes, sweetie," Eli said. "Ya look like yer about to bust a gut!"

His use of the expression only made it worse. "I'm fine, heh-heh, fine…continue, please…" she said in a high-pitched whisper.

Now Eli snorted.

"Oh good grief," Preacher Jo said and lost it.

That, of course, sent Pleasant over the edge. She began to cackle, which in turn pushed Eli into a belly laugh. Wilfred, who was sitting in the front pew, went next. Then the floodgates opened and the whole church followed.

Preacher Jo raised his arms and motioned for everyone to calm down, but it did no good—especially since he couldn't even calm himself. Pleasant was bent double at this point, tears streaming down her face. The laughter felt good, and the stress from weeks of fleeing from her family fell away. Eli was guffawing, leaning back to rattle the rafters. There was a thud as Mary Mulligan fell out of a pew and onto the floor, which took the hysterics up a notch.

After several minutes, with Eli's help, Pleasant straightened and grinned at Preacher Jo. The reverend managed to take a deep breath and wipe his eyes. "All right, calm down everyone!" he called. "Let's continue!"

The church slowly quieted. Eli tugged on his jacket and pulled at his collar, obviously not used to wearing such clothing. "I'll be hornswoggled—I didn't know ya could laugh like that," he whispered to Pleasant.

"Neither did I," Pleasant admitted. She took a deep breath and they both nodded at Preacher Jo.

"Thank Heaven," he replied. "All right, now that we've got that out of our systems, into this union Pleasant and Eli now come to be joined."

Wilfred began to chuckle again in the front pew. Irene nudged him with her elbow, but a few others picked it up.

"Stop, or we'll never get through this!" Preacher Jo demanded.

Unfortunately, a ripple of titters and giggles kept moving through the church. "Best just finish it, Preacher Jo!" Patrick Mulligan called.

Preacher Jo sighed, then said, "If any of you can

show just cause why they may not be lawfully wed, speak now or else forever hold your peace!" He snorted, once, but managed to stop himself.

"I do!" a voice shouted from the back of the church.

That started everyone laughing again, and several people looked around to see who the joker was. Some, including Pleasant and Eli, laughed louder.

"I said, I OBJECT!"

Everyone quieted and turned. Standing in the doorway at the back of the church was a man. No, make that, men. Several of them.

Pleasant turned and gasped. "Oh no…"

One of the men strode halfway up the aisle and glared at her. "Surprised to see us, dear sister?"

"Major!" She looked past him. "Michael? Matt? Darcy?" Her knees buckled. Thankfully Eli was there to catch her.

"What's the meaning of this?" Preacher Jo barked. "Who are you?"

Another man shoved his way past the first and marched to the front of the church. "I'll tell you who I am," he said in a thick Down East accent. "I'm Rupert Jerney, her betrothed!"

Pleasant took one look at him, screamed and, regaining her footing, hid behind Eli.

Rupert pulled out a gun and aimed it at him. "I'll ask you, sir, to let go of my fiancée."

"Yer fiancée?!" Eli said in shock. "What the Sam Hill are ya talkin' 'bout?"

Rupert quickly looked him up and down as the men behind him began to make their way down the aisle. "Why, you are nothing but a lowly country hick."

A series of *clicks* followed the remark as every man in the church cocked his gun and aimed it at the newcomer. His companions looked at the good townspeople of Clear Creek in shock, and backed up a few steps.

"No one calls my brother names," a voice said behind Rupert.

He turned, took one look at the sheriff's star pinned to the man's jacket and blanched. "She's mine, Sheriff. If you know what's good faw you, you'll stay out of this."

"Brother?" Major repeated. "She's marrying a lawman?"

"Yes, a deputy," Preacher Jo said. His gun was in his hand too, though no one had seen him draw it. He pointed it at Rupert. "Now, Mr. Rupert Jerney, I'd like to hear what Miss Comfort has to say about all this. I strongly suggest you keep your mouth shut while she does, or so help me, you'll wish I'd let Sheriff Turner arrest you."

"Arrest me?" Rupert sneered. "Faw what?"

"Disturbing the peace," Tom Turner replied. "Threatenin' folks with a deadly weapon."

"Being a conceited, arrogant blowhard!" Pleasant yelled from her refuge behind Eli.

"What did you call me?" Rupert hissed.

"Rupert?" one of the men with him said. "Our sister doesn't seem very glad to see you."

"Major!" Pleasant squeaked. "What are you doing here?"

"Rupert said you were in grave danger. He feared you'd been kidnapped."

"What?" she gasped.

"About sent our poor daddy to drinking," another said.

"Are these yer relations?" Eli asked.

"My brothers," she said. "All six of them."

"Six?" Preacher Jo echoed as he looked them over. "Well. Everyone, please put those guns away so we can settle this."

A shot was fired, then another. People dove for cover, then realized the reports were coming from outside.

"Tarnation!" Tom Turner looked at his brother. "The jail!"

No sooner had he said it than there was a loud BOOM!

"It's a jailbreak!" Eli shouted. He turned to Preacher Jo and shoved Pleasant into his arms. "Take care of her!" Ignoring Rupert and company, he joined his brother Tom.

Colin and Harrison Cooke jumped to their feet, their pistols still trained on the newcomers. "We'll handle things here," Harrison told the Turners. "Go!"

Tom and Eli ran for the church doors as fast as they could, with Bran O'Hare right behind. They had over a dozen prisoners locked up, with only Henry Fig to guard them. To have them all loose at once could cause a lot of damage, not to mention the ones that done the loosing.

Other men began to follow, guns at the ready, as the realization of what could happen hit them. "We'll help!" several cried as they followed the Turners and Bran outside.

Colin and Harrison took Pleasant from Preacher Jo and pushed her behind them. "Now let's all calm down and settle this," Colin suggested. "I do believe a posse is about to form, so I suggest you talk fast."

More shots echoed outside, followed by the sound of galloping horses. Pleasant's brothers glanced between

Rupert and the church doors. "How many are escaping?" Major asked.

"There were at least a dozen outlaws locked up at the sheriff's office," Wilfred explained. "Could be more than twice that now what with their cohorts busting them out."

"More than a dozen?!" Major glanced around the church. His eyes locked on Honoria for a moment before he faced the Cooke brothers. "Who knows what they'll do? Are these all the women and children?"

"No, some folks left after church to go tend to things at home," explained Preacher Jo. "They'd planned to come back to town for the wedding supper."

"You mean the whole town is here?" Darcy asked.

"Yes," Pleasant stifled a sob. "Because they care about each other here. They care about me. And you all had to come along and ruin everything!"

Her brothers stared at her a moment. "So it seems," Major said. He glared a dagger at Rupert. "We'll deal with you later." He turned back to Colin and Harrison. "Sirs, three of us served in the Confederate Army during the war, and all of us are trained with firearms. If you'll have us, we'd be glad to help."

More shots, closer this time, followed by a woman's shriek. "That sounded like Grandma!" Preacher Jo said, his features locked in panic.

"Grandma?" Pleasant came out from behind the Cooke brothers. "We've got to help her!"

"Grandma?" Rupert spat and tried to grab her arm. "I don't care about some silly old bat in this hayseed town! You're coming with me!"

Major sapped him on the back of the head with the

butt of his pistol, sending him to the floor out cold. "No, she's not, you lying Yankee!"

Colin and Harrison exchanged a quick glance. "We have no idea what's going on between you and your sister," Harrison told Major. "But if you and your brothers can help with the current crisis, come with us."

Major and his brothers nodded. "What about that lying snake Rupert?" one of them asked.

Major looked at Preacher Jo. "Would you be so kind as to tie this muggins up for us? We'll be back to deal with him later."

Preacher Jo nodded. "Best get out there and help, gentlemen." He looked at the older men that remained. "We'll stay and protect the women and children. And deal with—" He waved his gun at the prone Rupert. "—him. Wilfred, Patrick, I've got a length of rope back in the church office—could you do the honors?"

"Be happy to, lad."

"We'll have him hogtied in two shakes." The men went to get the rope.

Colin and Harrison motioned for the others to follow them. They hurried out of the church to their horses, the Cooke brothers mounting up behind two of the Comfort brothers, and headed toward the shooting.

Pleasant sank to the floor. Sadie and Belle ran to her side, got her to her feet and guided her to a pew. "Are you all right?" Belle asked.

"No, I'm not all right! My husband just ran out the door to get himself shot at!"

"He's not your husband yet," Sadie reminded her. "But he will be as soon as they round up those outlaws."

Rupert began to stir and moan. Preacher Jo sighed, bent over him and, as soon as the dandy raised his head and started to rise, whacked him on the occipital again. He went down like a felled steer. "Sadie's right—we'll finish the ceremony as soon as the men return." He looked at the unconscious Rupert. "Who is this anyway?"

Pleasant sighed wearily. "The reason I left Savannah."

"Doc Waller!" Eli cried as he dove beside him behind a horse trough. "What are ya and Grandma doin' out here?"

"We were heading to the church from the hotel. Grandma wanted to get a few last-minute pies done so she could set them on the food tables with the rest. Made us late for the wedding. We were heading to the church when the dynamite went off!"

"Then what happened?"

"Your prisoners started legging it out of there. I told Grandma to head for the church while I turned for the sheriff's office. I knew Henry was there and I had to make sure he was all right."

"Where's he now?"

"In the saloon, all shook up but no worse for wear. I imagine he and a few of them outlaws have a headache from the noise. Once they can hear again, that is."

"Tarnation!" Eli exclaimed. He peeked over the top of the trough. There wasn't a man in sight. The outlaws had scattered, but whoever broke them out didn't take into consideration they'd need horses for all of them. Half got to ride away, but the rest were hiding around town, and one of them must've seen Grandma heading for the church and grabbed her. Where were they now?

"Stay low," Eli said. "I don't want ya to get yerself taken hostage too."

"Get my Sarah back, Eli," Doc Waller said, tears in his eyes. "This is all my fault. I should've kept her with me!"

Eli nodded. "I will, sir." He got up and ran for the saloon doors. Several shots were fired and a bullet shattered a window. Aha—some of the varmints were still in the sheriff's office!

He took cover inside, crouched beneath the broken window and slowly peeked over the sill. One side of the sheriff's office was in tatters—they'd blown part of a wall out. He wondered how many of their gang the dynamite took with it. One thing was for sure— the outlaws had raided the building's store of guns and ammunition. What else would they be using to shoot at him?

"Dagnabit!" he said, wondering where Tom was. They'd split up—Tom had mounted his horse and taken off after the escaped prisoners galloping out of town, while Eli had gone to check on Henry. That's when he noticed Doc Waller diving for cover by Mulligan's Saloon.

"What a wedding day," he muttered to himself. And even once they took care of the outlaws, he had a thing or two to settle back at the church. Maybe he should never have left.

Chapter Sixteen

"He lied, Major! He's been lying the entire time!" Darcy complained to his older brother.

"We never should've left Daddy in Denver with Aunt Phidelia," Michael said. "He'd want to be here."

"He's better off where he is," said Major. "The old man's not in his right mind—the best place for him is with our aunt. We'll deal with Rupert as soon as we're done here."

Colin and Harrison listened to the Comfort brothers' heated argument and were quickly able to piece together what brought them to Clear Creek. What they hadn't figured out was why two of the brothers were calling the eldest Major, while the others referred to him as Quince. Maybe "Quince" had been a major in the Confederate Army...that would explain it.

"You of all people should have seen this coming," another remarked—Matt, perhaps? There were so many of them it was hard to keep track.

"I had my suspicions, but I wanted to see for myself. The fact of the matter is, my dear brothers, we've lost Comfort Fields and everything we hold dear. The only thing we haven't lost is each other. That should be more important than a big ol' house and a dwindling bank account, most of which belong to our father anyway."

"We all contributed," Zachary snapped. At least Harrison and Colin thought it was Zachary.

"And we all lost," Major pointed out.

"Yes, on account of our sister's selfishness," Matt (?) muttered under his breath.

"And if you'd been asked to marry an heiress with the temperament of a turnip and the looks of a potato, *Peaceful*, just so *we* could go on living the way we were accustomed, would you have done it?"

"I'd have made do," he remarked coolly.

"Only because you'd have kept a mistress on the side," Darcy said with a glare. "As would any of us if we were honest with ourselves. But that's not an option for Pleasant, now is it?"

Harrison and Colin exchanged a sage look. So *that's* why Pleasant became a mail-order bride. "This is all very well and good," Colin said, "but perhaps we should concentrate on the current crisis?"

No sooner had he said it than a shot rang out. They'd gotten as far as the livery stable after their gallop from the church. The bulk of the shootout was going on between the saloon and the sheriff's office.

"You're quite right," Major said. He looked at his brothers. "Michael, Darcy, Zachary—circle around the building and try to pin those Yankees down." He glanced at Colin and Harrison. "No offense."

"None taken," Harrison said with a shrug of indifference.

The three Comfort brothers gave Major a quick nod,

crept to the edge of the livery stable wall and peeked around it. Darcy motioned to the other two to follow him, and the remainder watched as they made their way toward the sheriff's office. Or what was left of it—a huge hole had been made from the dynamite used to break the outlaws out. Several of the outlaws hadn't survived it.

Harrison, Colin and "Peaceful" Matt made their way to the other end of the livery stable. They stayed close to the wall and edged their way around to the front of the building. Once Michael, Darcy and Zachary flushed the outlaws out of the sheriff's office, they could spring on them and round them up.

"I hope Eli figures out what we're doing," Harrison said quietly.

"Don't worry, he's smart enough to see what we're about," Colin assured.

"Eli...that's the man our sister was about to marry?" Matt asked.

"Yes," Harrison said. "And you couldn't ask for a better man for your sister. I strongly suggest you give her your blessing."

"He's a good man, then?"

"As good as they come in our book," Colin said. "In fact, it might interest you to know that he's a hero in these parts, as is his brother Tom, the sheriff."

"I hear lawmen out here are good at turning wives into widows," Matt remarked flatly.

"Anything can turn a wife into a widow around here, dear sir," Harrison said. "But enough of this talk—we have outlaws to capture."

"But what about...?" Matt never got to finish. It was then that the real shooting started.

* * *

Preacher Jo tightened the rope that Wilfred and Patrick had used to bind Rupert's wrists, then did the same with the knots at his ankles. "There, that ought to hold you."

Rupert moved his jaw this way and that. "I thought that you being a man of God, you'd know bettah than to strike a gentleman. You're going to pay for that, preachah."

"He'll pay for nothing, Rupert," Pleasant snapped. "How dare you show up like this!"

"How dare you run away from me," he sneered. "Your daddy and I had an agreement."

"I was not informed of it. Your agreement means nothing to me."

"You selfish, foolish girl. Your family lost everything because of you."

"Maybe I should gag him," Preacher Jo mused, rubbing his chin.

"No, *my* family lost everything because *you* didn't see it in your heart to help my father when he asked for it. After all, it would've been the neighborly thing to do. We'd have helped your family out if your mills weren't doing well."

"Neighbuhly?" Rupert hissed, ignoring everything else she said. "What fool-headed nonsense is this? I do what I do to get what I want. If your daddy was fool enough to borrow money from me, he should've known what he was getting himself into."

"He expected you to do the right thing," Pleasant shot back. "Not be forced to…to…use me to pay off his loan."

Rupert's smile was demonic. "And sell you he did,

my deah, along with everything else. I now own your precious Comfort Fields, lock, stock and barrel. All because he failed to deliver you. However… I'd be willing to be a bit moah—what did you call it?—neighbuhly if you'll stop this nonsense and come back with me."

Pleasant's mouth fell open. "Are you out of your mind? I'm not leaving Clear Creek!"

Rupert twisted his body and looked over his shoulder at the townspeople that remained, then turned back to her. "You mean you'd rather live out heah in this wilderness with a bunch of lowlife hicks?"

Patrick Mulligan charged at him, but Preacher Jo caught him by the arm. "Don't, Paddy. He's not worth it."

"I won't let that snobbish dandy call us names without a fight!"

Wilfred stepped forward. "Yeah, who does he think he is?"

"Everyone just calm down," Preacher Jo ordered. "Let's concentrate on making sure we're all safe. Don't let this witless worm distract you."

"Mighty derogatory wuhds, coming from a preachah," Rupert sneered.

"I'd be quiet if I were you," Preacher Jo warned.

"Let me give him just one," Patrick made a fist. "Right in the puss! Just one, Preacher Jo!"

Preacher Jo sighed. "Might I remind you of what the Good Book says about loving our enemies?"

"I'll patch him up after. That would be loving, aye?"

Rupert began to cackle. "You people are so stupid, you can't even decide whethah or not to hit me. How pathetic and weak." He narrowed his eyes at Pleasant. "And *you* were about to marry one of these insects?"

Preacher Jo sighed. "All right, Paddy. Just one."

Patrick Mulligan grinned, promptly turned and punched Rupert right in the mouth. There was a sickening crack that made the women gasp.

"Better?" Preacher Jo asked dryly.

"Aye—that felt bonny!" Patrick said, still smiling. Behind him, Wilfred laughed wheezily.

Rupert spit out a couple pieces of tooth and glared viciously at them. "Why you duhty, yellow-bellied, sorry excuse for a preachah!"

Preacher Jo bent down, looked him in the eye and said, "I wasn't always a man of God, son."

"That's right!" Wilfred said with a laugh. "Preacher Jo is one of the fastest guns in these parts—next to our beloved Turner brothers, of course."

Rupert seemed to finally realize his true predicament. He glanced at Patrick, his meaty Irish hands balled into fists, then at the quick-draw preacher and finally the rest of the townsfolk of Clear Creek, who glared at him like a lynch mob. If he wasn't careful, they'd probably string him up. He audibly gulped and laid back down on the floor.

"And," Preacher Jo added, "I think we're all tired of hearing your voice, *sir*." Quick as a flash, he stuffed a handkerchief in Rupert's mouth, then tied it in place with another.

Pleasant look down at him and shook her head. "You should have stayed in Savannah, Rupert. You'd have been a lot safer there."

Bound and now gagged, Rupert swallowed hard. At the moment, he had little choice but to agree.

The outlaws hunkered down in the jail—those still alive anyway—had been chained up. Now all that was left was to aid Tom in rescuing Grandma and capturing the rest. Eli shook his head in disgust as he noted the crumpled wall of the sheriff's office, not to mention the crumpled outlaws decorating it. "Fools." He'd examined them and was relieved the young man whose horse he was keeping wasn't among them. Unfortunately, now he'd suffer the same fate as the rest for running.

"We're ready, Eli," Harrison said as he rode up to him.

Eli examined his mount. "Ya sure ya wanna ride like that?"

Harrison shifted on his horse. "In the heat of the moment, this is all Colin and I have. We just unhitched them from the wagon. Don't worry, we're both quite adept at riding bareback."

"So long as it don't interrupt yer shootin', I'm fine with it." He mounted his own horse.

"What do you want us to do?" Pleasant's eldest brother asked as he joined them.

Eli turned in his saddle to face him. "Much obliged to ya for askin'."

"My brothers and I have no problem towing the mark."

Eli nodded his thanks. "For now, follow me. My guess is they're headin' straight for the tree line where they can keep outta sight and see us comin'."

"Very well, then." He nodded at his brothers.

Eli repositioned his horse so he was parallel with him. "Deputy Eli Turner." He offered him his hand.

He shook it. "Major Quincy Comfort, at your service."

Eli smiled. "What do I call ya?"

Major stared at him a moment, then his eyebrows

rose as realization dawned. "Young sir, will you be a good husband for my sister?"

"Sir, I'll do everythin' I can for her—even lay down my life if it comes to that."

Major smiled. "Deputy...then that means you'll be family. And family calls me Quince."

Eli tipped his hat. "Well then, Quince, let's go rescue us a damsel in distress and round up some outlaws. Yee-haw!" He kicked his horse and was off like a shot, with Harrison, Colin and several others quick to follow.

"Quince," Benedict said as they got their horses moving. "Did you mean it when you said we have a new member in the family?"

"Yes, I did, gentlemen," he said. "Now let's ride."

It didn't take much to track Tom and the other men. When they caught up, the earlier group was hiding amidst the same outcropping of rocks where he and Eli had first captured the varmints. "Talk about returnin' to the scene of the crime," Eli said with a shake of his head. He looked at his brother. "What do ya suppose they left behind?"

"Had to be somethin' important for 'em to come back here. Maybe stolen loot, who knows?" Tom noticed Eli's posse. "Afternoon, folks."

The Comfort men tipped their hats. "Good afternoon," they replied quietly.

"Seems we got a bit of a problem," Tom said. "They got Grandma Waller as a hostage."

"We know," said Eli. "Doc saw 'em take her. How many are there?"

"I'd say about a dozen and a half."

"That many?!" Eli blew out a breath. "Tarnation—then at least six came to break 'em out."

"That's what I came up with too. Gotta figger Snake, Frog and Lizard are among 'em."

The Comfort brothers stopped examining their surroundings and turned to them.

"We know—bunch of idiot names," Eli said.

Quince nodded and looked like he was trying not to smile. "Some of us are quite familiar with that sort of thing."

Eli smiled anyway. "I can imagine."

Quince joined him in his amusement and the two began to chuckle.

"Glad to see ya've gotten chummy," Tom said. "Now let's get down to business. Grandma must be scared to death. The sooner we take care of this, the sooner we can get back to the church."

"The church?" Matt said.

Quince rolled his eyes. "Have you forgotten our sister is getting married today?"

The young man sighed. "No."

Quince gave the Turner brothers a solemn nod. "He'll come around. Now let's do this."

Eli and Tom nodded in agreement. It was time to catch some outlaws.

Preacher Jo, Patrick, Wilfred and the rest of the men left behind had posted guards at the doors leading into the sanctuary and the one from the church office outside. No one moved until Doc Drake came and let everyone know that the town had been secured and a posse had taken off after the remaining outlaws.

"Where are my brothers?" Pleasant asked.

"They went with Eli and the Cookes," Doc Drake told her. "Don't worry, they'll be back."

Her hand automatically went to her mouth as she fought a sob. Her anger at Rupert for chasing her across the country and showing up to ruin her wedding, not to mention what he'd done to her family, had dissipated. Now every man she cared about, save her father, was out there risking their life to save Grandma Waller and capture a bunch of bloodthirsty brigands.

Half-witted, bloodthirsty brigands, from the sounds of it. Everyone in town now knew the idiots had blown a huge hole in one wall of the sheriff's office, only to kill some of their own men. Doc Drake and a few others had seen to the dead and were now in the church, taking care of wounded townspeople. Doc Waller was the worst off among the residents, though, and he'd only gotten a few scrapes and bruises.

But would Eli and his posse be as lucky? Would everyone come back unharmed, or would she lose one or more of them? She couldn't bear it if she did. Her anger at Rupert had blinded her to how much she'd missed her brothers. Their offer to help Eli and the others track down the outlaws also reminded her that, at their core, they were honorable men. Rupert must have spun quite a tale to get them to come along after her. Unless they'd come for another reason…

"Doc Drake! Come quick!" Wilfred cried from his post at the church doors. Most of Clear Creek's residents had stayed there, feeling it safer than wandering around town or trying to make for home.

"What is it?" he asked as he hurried down the church aisle to the door.

"Look!" Wilfred pointed.

Doc Drake squinted. "Well, I'll be—it's Grandma!"

Chapter Seventeen

❧

"Yeah, but who's that with her?" Wilfred asked. "I don't recognize the horse or the rider."

"Preacher Jo!" Doc Drake called over his shoulder.

Preacher Jo ran to join them, gun drawn, and peered at the approaching horse. Grandma rode in front of a man. "That looks like one of the outlaws."

Other guns were immediately drawn and cocked. Doc Drake turned and waved his hands at them. "Calm yourselves. Preacher Jo and I will handle this."

"Is Grandma all right?" Cyrus Van Cleet asked.

Doc Drake glanced out the door. "She looks fine. Now stay put, everyone." He stepped outside, unarmed, and waited. Preacher Jo joined him, gun still in hand.

Grandma gripped the saddle horn as the horse trotted up to the church. "Land sakes, Preacher, put that shootin' iron away!" she scolded.

Preacher Jo did, and exchanged a quick look with Doc Drake. "Grandma? Are you all right?" he asked.

"Thanks to this youngun, I am. He got me away from those bandits and we escaped together."

"Escaped?" Doc Drake said as the youth brought the horse to a stop in front of them.

"Yessir," he said. "My brother Teddy forced me to go with 'em when Lizard blowed the jail up. I told 'im I didn't wanna and I don't want no part of thievin' no more. So he took the old lady to make me do what he wanted."

Preacher Jo helped Grandma off the horse as the boy jumped down. "You must be Ninian."

"Yessir, Ninian Rush. My brother's the big fella, Ted Rush. Teddy, I call 'im."

Preacher Jo put a hand on the youth's shoulder. "What you did was very brave, Ninian. You rescued a kidnapped woman. We'll see to it that Judge Whipple takes that into account when he gets here tomorrow."

"Tomorry?!" the youth croaked and swallowed hard.

"Now don't go getting yourself worked up over nothing," Grandma said. "If it weren't for you I wouldn't be here."

"How did you get away?" Doc Drake asked.

"I pertended to join up again," Ninian said with a shrug. "Teddy ordered me to haul 'er up to this burnt-out ol' cabin to wait for him 'n the others. 'Stead we got on a horse 'n rode here."

Doc Drake and Preacher Jo stared at them for a second before they both burst out laughing.

"Yeah…guess it is kinda funny," Ninian said shyly. Then he noted the crowd behind them with guns drawn and gulped. "Y'ain't mad at me, are ya?"

"Of course not," said Preacher Jo. "You were forced to go with them, and you did what you had to do to protect Grandma. For that the town is grateful." He turned to the townspeople. "Isn't that right?"

Guns were shoved back into holsters as the residents of Clear Creek nodded and murmured their agreement. Ninian watched them and sighed in relief.

Pleasant made her way to them. "What about Eli and my brothers?"

"Couldn't say, ma'am. Grandma 'n I left just as they got thar. Teddy 'n the others were tryna figger out what to do."

"They'll be back." Grandma put an arm around her. "If I can survive a gang of outlaws, how much more so the deputy and sheriff?"

Pleasant smiled weakly and let herself be ushered back inside. Doc Drake followed.

Preacher Jo turned back to Ninian. "Let's go into my office. I have something I'd like to talk with you about."

"What?"

Preacher Jo smiled. "What if I can fix it with the judge so you have to help me out around here?"

Ninian's face scrunched up in confusion. "Help out?"

"Call it community service. It would beat going back to jail, wouldn't it? You did a brave thing saving Grandma, but the judge might still want you to serve some kind of sentence."

"Ya mean I'd be workin' for ya? Heck, preacher. That ain't no sentence, that'd be a pleasure!"

Preacher Jo smiled. "Not a pleasure, Ninian. A blessing."

Several hours went by, and still no sign of the posse. Pleasant was beside herself, pacing in the hotel lobby. Polly Van Cleet, a petite woman with a bright countenance, had suggested the bride and the wedding guests—in this case, almost the whole town—take advantage of the wedding supper that had been laid out. The hotel dining room was filled with people eating, drinking and trying their best to be merry under the circumstances.

"He'll be fine, Miss Comfort," Lorcan Brody said from his post behind the counter. "You'll see."

"How can you know? How can anyone know?" She wrung her handkerchief in her hands. "We haven't heard a word."

"If anyone was really hurt, one of them would've come back to fetch Doc Drake."

She spun on him. "One man! He's only one man!"

"Aye, but he's the best man if someone's hurt."

She stopped and looked at the ceiling. "Of course, he's the town doctor. But what if more than one man is hurt?"

Lorcan smiled. "Then the good doctor has more than one patient to deal with. He's done it before. And he has Doc Waller to help him."

She looked at him. "I'm sorry. This has been a trying day." She studied the man behind the counter. He was looking right at her, his warm smile still in place. Perfectly normal, except she knew he couldn't see.

She turned toward the dining room and watched the people of Clear Creek eat and chat. Rupert looked like just another wedding guest, except for being tied to a chair and looking very cross. Irene Dunnigan sat right next to him, ladle in hand, occasionally taking a bite from the plate in front of her but otherwise looking just as perturbed. Every time Rupert spat out a nasty remark, she'd clobbered him with the ladle. Eventually he figured it out and was now being very quiet.

"Clear Creek," Pleasant whispered to herself. It was

a town full of quirky and occasionally irritating residents, but she found the wacky mix had started to grow on her. She suspected she'd have a hard time returning to life in Savannah even if she wanted to.

She again turned to Lorcan behind the counter... and found him *writing*! How could a blind man write with pen and ink? He acted as if he wasn't blind at all, yet everyone assured her he was. It seemed uncanny.

But then there was Grandma Waller, old enough to be everyone's grandmother yet had gumption to spare. The Mulligans owned the town saloon, yet served more food than whiskey. The town doctor, she was beginning to suspect, had more than just medical knowledge that helped people get well—people seemed to imply he had some divine gift. And all the Cookes, high-born English men and women now living out west. Everyone out here was some kind of oddity.

And then there was Eli Turner, her betrothed. Living in a tiny shack in the boondocks, barely able to speak the King's English...and half of a team of heroes who was even now out on the prairie somewhere, risking life and limb for the sake of this little town. "And me," she added softly.

Her eyes drifted once more to the dining room and the people in it. Clear Creek was now her town; these were the folks she'd call friends and neighbors. She smiled. For all their strangeness, they were the kindest, most caring, bravest people she had ever known. And once she married Eli, she'd be one of them—if she wasn't already. The runaway from Georgia, one more oddity among the rest.

She closed her eyes and smiled. "And proud of it," she said to herself.

Lorcan's head came up. "Ye're missing yer wedding supper, Miss Comfort."

Pleasant looked at him and smiled. "You're right—I should go in. Would you care to join me, Mr. Brody?"

He stood up and stretched. "Don't mind if I do."

Pleasant watched him walk around the counter and come right to her. "How do you do that?"

He smiled. "Practice." He offered her his arm. "Shall we?"

She smiled, took his arm and let *him* lead *her* into the hotel dining room.

They'd no sooner entered when Honoria Cooke ran into the hotel and then the dining room, panting like a winded horse. "Here they come!" she shouted. "They're…they're back!"

"Honoria!" Sadie said. "Where have you been all this time?"

"I posted myself…as lookout." She bent over, hands on her knees, sucking in air. Her hair was a mess, the skirt of her dress torn and dirty. She looked as if she'd been up a tree, and maybe had.

Henry Fig moseyed in next, also shouting the news—and almost got run over by the townspeople hurrying out. "Wait! Hey—I'm trying to tell you…!"

"Hush up, dear!" Fanny called back. "We already heard!"

Henry rolled his eyes. "Well, consarnit, that just figures!"

"Oh, don't worry about it, hon. Come here and have something to eat."

When everyone reached the street they saw Eli and Tom Turner leading a ragtag group of bandits, roped together much as they had been the first time they were caught, the infamous Lizard Grunsky and company among them. The Comfort brothers brought up the rear, one listing to one side on his horse as they did.

"Quince!" Pleasant cried and ran toward them. She stopped short at Eli's horse.

He nodded to her brother. "Yeah, he got hisself shot."

His casual tone startled her. "You don't have to sound so…so blasé about it!"

"I ain't bein'…well, whatever ya just said, sweetie. I'm tired and…" Now Eli slumped.

"Eli!"

Tom rode up alongside his brother and pulled him up straight, while Harrison quickly unwrapped the rope used to lead their prisoners from around Eli's saddle horn and gripped it in his hand. "Tom, take them both to Doc Drake. Hurry! The rest of us will see to these chaps."

"Eli?" Pleasant cried as Tom jumped from his horse onto the back of Eli's. She then looked at her brothers. "What happened?"

"We were trying to flush them out into the open," Benedict explained.

"A few of them managed to sneak behind us," Colin added as he rode up.

Darcy turned in his saddle and glared at the outlaws. "Quince spotted them, shouted a warning and got a bullet in the shoulder for his trouble."

"Eli tried to protect him and took one low, just above the hip," Harrison said. "I have to commend your brothers, Pleasant. They fought bravely and valiantly."

"Merciful heavens!" She watched as Tom headed down the street toward the doctors', gripping her betrothed to keep him on the horse.

Major followed with Michael assisting. "Your Eli is lucky it went clean through," said Michael. "We patched him up as best we could. I hate to be the one to inform you, dear sister, but your future husband is as stubborn as a mule. He insisted he finish his job and haul his prisoners back to town."

"He's lost a lot of blood by now," Major said weakly.

"Both of you have." Colin maneuvered his horse next to his. "You need to get to Doc Drake straight away."

"I'm right here, Colin," Doc Drake made his way through the crowd. "But yes, get him to the house. I'll take things from there."

Michael handed Colin his reins, climbed from his own horse to behind the saddle of Major's, put an arm around his waist to keep him from falling off his mount and took off down the street at a canter.

Honoria, meanwhile, took Pleasant by the shoulders. "Come on, let's follow."

Pleasant nodded numbly as Honoria led her to the doctors' house. Both her intended and her brother were wounded. What if they were worse off than they looked? She bit her lower lip and willed herself not to cry as she headed down the street.

"He's lost a lot of blood, Bowen," Doc Waller commented to Doc Drake as he examined Eli's wound.

Bowen Drake deftly examined Pleasant's brother. "So has this one. Let's see what we can do to get them patched up."

They had both men in the patient room at the back of the house. Thankfully they had two beds; otherwise Eli and Major would have had to share.

"Where's Pleasant?" Eli asked, weakly.

"Waiting in the parlor with Grandma," Doc Waller told him. "You sit tight son, you're not going anywhere."

"The wedding…"

"…can wait. This gunshot wound can't." He turned to Bowen. "Hand me those bandages, will you?"

Bowen did, then went back to work on his patient.

"I'm sorry we ruined your wedding, Mr. Turner," Major said through gritted teeth.

"Hold still," Bowen ordered. "I have to get this bullet out."

"Well, as I see it," Eli rasped, "them outlaws done most of that." He turned his head to look at him. "I guess all things work for good like the Almighty says. If ya hadn't shown up and helped us recapture the varmints, we might never have made it back alive."

Major winced in pain as Doc Drake did his work, then glanced at Eli. "The woman…she's safe?"

"Will you two shut it?" Doc Waller snapped. "Land sakes, you've both been shot, for crying out loud. Stay quiet and let us work!"

Major and Eli closed their eyes and did as they were told.

"And for your information, Grandma is fine and serving tea in the parlor," Doc Waller informed them. "That young feller you had locked up before, Eli, he brought her back to town safe and sound."

Eli smiled despite the pain. "I knew he'd do right."

"Thank the Lord he did." Bowen pulled the bullet from Major's shoulder and dropped it into a metal pan with a *clink*. "He said his brother forced him to go with them when they were broken out. They took Grandma as leverage to make sure Ninian would do as he was told."

Eli managed to smile despite the grimace on his face. "I like that boy. Gotta a fine horse too…"

"Shush!" Doc Waller ordered. "Don't waste your strength talking."

Eli smiled weakly and closed his eyes, his head lolling to one side. This time, he didn't reopen them for a while.

Chapter Eighteen

"What's taking them so long?" Pleasant asked as she paced the parlor.

"For Heaven's sake, child, sit down and finish your tea," Grandma said. "All that walking isn't going to do you a bit of good."

"You can't blame her, Grandma," Honoria said. "If my future husband was in there, I'd probably be pacing too."

Grandma sighed in resignation. "This day has been a doozy, hasn't it?"

Honoria studied the torn hem of her dress. "Yes, it certainly has."

Doc Waller suddenly burst into the parlor. "Er…ah…" He looked between the women. "Honoria, can I borrow you for a minute?"

"What's going on?" Grandma asked. "Do I need to help?"

"You've been through enough for one day, Sarah. Besides, I need a stronger pair of hands. Honoria can handle it."

Honoria swallowed hard. "If you say so, Doc. What do you need me to do?"

"Come with me." He turned and hurried back to the patient room in the rear of the house.

Honoria's eyes darted between Grandma and Pleasant. She took a deep breath, shrugged, got up and followed him.

"What's that about?" Pleasant asked worriedly.

Grandma shook her head. "One of them must be bleeding pretty bad. I have no idea which one."

A hand flew to Pleasant's mouth as her jaw began to tremble. "Oh, Grandma! I can't lose Eli or Major! I just can't!"

Grandma stood up and pulled Pleasant into her arms. "There now, child. Doc and Bowen will do everything they can to make sure both your men pull out of this."

"But what if they can't? What if one of them dies?"

"Don't go jumping to conclusions, child. We don't know what's going on back there. And if, God forbid, the good Lord takes one of them, then we'll do what we have to do. Dying is part of living—that's just the way things are. You'll see your share of it in this world, no doubt about it."

Pleasant pulled away to wipe the tears from her eyes. "I've never had to deal with death, other than my mother. But I can hardly count that—she died giving birth to my brother and me, so I never knew her. I guess… I guess I never had to deal with much of anything until now." More tears fell.

Grandma stroked her hair tenderly. "Then ain't you glad you got friends and folks here that can help see you through it?"

Pleasant stared at her. She was right—she did have friends here. The people of Clear Creek stood by each other, she'd seen them do it. And there were her brothers on top of that. She took a deep breath to stop her tears, then hugged Grandma. "Thank you for reminding me of that. And thank you for being with me now."

"You're part of this town, Pleasant. Of course I'm gonna be with you. Now sit down and finish your cup of tea before it gets cold. It'll calm your nerves."

Pleasant sniffled, went to the settee and sat. She picked up her teacup and took a slow sip of the hot brew. Grandma was right, it felt good going down her throat. A shiver went up her spine. This day *had* been a doozy—and it wasn't over yet.

"What's he doing?" Major Quincy Comfort asked, eyes wide, as he watched Bowen Drake close his eyes and put his hands over Eli's wound.

Honoria studied him as she pondered the man's name. She'd never heard of someone named "Major" before. "Doing what he does best," she replied.

"Let him have another swig of whiskey, Honoria," Doc Waller ordered.

She handed Major a flask. He took it gratefully and gulped a few mouthfuls, grimacing as he handed it back to her. "I've never been much of a drinking man…"

"Good for you, son," Doc Waller replied. "How'd you break a rib?"

Major let his head fall back against the pillow. "Eli tackled me to get me…out of the way. I landed on a sharp rock. Eli landed on…his side on top of me. That's…when he was hit."

Doc continued to stitch up his shoulder. "It's a good thing too, or you'd be dead. That bullet probably would've caught you right in the gut. I'm just glad you two made it back alive so we could tend you proper."

Major glanced at Eli, Bowen still bent over him. "He's lost too much blood."

"He'll pull through," Doc assured him.

"How can you be sure?"

Doc looked at Bowen. "Because I've seen it before. Now hold still, I'm not done yet. Honoria, bring me some bandages from the hutch over there—I'm gonna teach you how to wrap some ribs."

She nodded and obeyed. She saw Major Comfort (good heavens, what a name!) watching her, and met his gaze as she returned to her chair by the bed, bandages in hand.

"Just hang onto those while I finish this," Doc said.

She complied and sat quietly. Major kept his gaze locked on her, and she tried not to fidget under his scrutiny. The man had been shot, after all, and might have a broken rib to boot. Who knew what was going on in his mind...

"Do you have brothers?"

Honoria jumped. "What?"

Major swallowed hard and licked his dry lips. "Do you have brothers?"

She studied his brown hair with golden highlights from the sun. "Yes. But you shouldn't be talking—you'll only waste your strength."

"I've suffered as much before," he said.

Honoria shook her head. "That seems unlikely."

"Don't be too sure," Doc Waller replied. "He's got a scar on his other shoulder to match this one."

Major nodded slightly. "Got hit by a Union bullet... guarding a rail line south of Waynesboro. Trying to stop Sherman's March to the Sea. I didn't quite succeed," he added with a chuckle.

"Oh my!" Honoria gasped. This man was a war hero…well, on the wrong side of the war, she thought, but nonetheless.

"But it's my sister's betrothed I'm worried about. I won't see her made a widow so soon."

"She won't be," Honoria said. "They never got the chance to finish the wedding, remember?"

"Oh yes," he said weakly. "My brothers and I interrupted it."

"You and them dang-blasted outlaws," Doc Waller tossed in.

"Maybe if you hadn't, they'd have gotten to the 'I do's' before the outlaws broke out," Honoria said.

"Perhaps." He turned his head to see what Doc Waller was doing. "Give me that flask again, Miss… ?"

"Cooke," she told him.

"Miss Cooke." He seemed weaker. Or tired, she wasn't sure which. It was amazing the man was talking at all, considering he'd only had but a few swigs of whiskey as painkiller while Doc Drake dug a bullet out of him and Doc Waller closed him up. She handed him the flask.

But he didn't bring it to his lips. "Help the man, Honoria," Doc Waller ordered. "He's a sturdy thing, but every tree can only take so much wind before it starts to go over."

She helped him drink, then placed the flask on the table next to him. The poor man needed rest—riding back to town must have taken its toll on him.

She looked at Eli. Doc Drake sat quietly watching him before he reached for some of the bandages on the bed. "Honoria," he said. "Can you help me?"

She glanced at Doc Waller who nodded for her to go

ahead. She placed the bandages she held in her lap on the table, then got up and went around to the other bed.

"I need you to help me bandage his wound," he said. "We're going to have to wrap them around him." She nodded as he showed her what to do so they could get the job done.

As they worked she caught little glimpses of their other patient. He never took his eyes off her, and it made her nervous. The man might be weak and tired from blood loss and in pain, but his steady gaze had nothing to do with weakness and everything to do with interest.

Honoria swallowed hard as she watched him in return for a moment, then turned back to her work.

"How's our brother?" Darcy asked Pleasant as he and the rest of their siblings entered the parlor.

"I don't know," she said.

"I'll go check," Grandma said. "Pleasant, why don't you get your brothers some tea? Cups and saucers are in the dining room hutch. The kettle's on the stove and the tea is on the worktable. And bring them the cookie jar—it's full."

Pleasant nodded numbly. Perhaps the simple task would jolt her back to reality—if she wanted any part of reality right now. She took the teapot, went into the kitchen and began to prepare another pot.

Michael followed her. "I'm sorry, Pleasant."

She looked at him. "For what?"

"For ruining your wedding, for one. For listening to that swindler Rupert. For...not protecting you, when I should have," he finished haltingly.

"I ran away before you had the chance." She turned to get the cookie jar.

"We're all sorry, you know."

She reached for the jar. "Rupert must have told you quite the tale."

"He made it sound like you needed rescuing."

"And you believed him?"

Michael absently rubbed the stumps on his right hand. "We believed Major and Daddy."

She turned around, the jar in her hands. His eyes were full of regret. "You came a long way to rescue me."

"We came a long way to help Rupert bring you back to Savannah. But in truth, I think Major and the rest of us just wanted to see that you were okay."

She turned to him, setting the jar on the worktable harder than she needed to. "And what would you have done if you'd found me already married?"

Her brother took a step back, his mouth half-open to answer. She knew he was thinking of what to say. "None of us were sure what we'd find when we caught up to you."

"Aunt Phidelia told you where I was?"

"Yes. That matchmaker certainly didn't."

Pleasant couldn't help but smile. "Mrs. Pettigrew."

"That's her. She's a strange one."

"Eccentric," she corrected.

"Regardless, she wouldn't tell us anything."

"I imagine Aunt Phidelia finally relented because she thought I'd be married by the time you showed up."

"We thought so too, which is why we wondered why Rupert was so adamant."

Her eyes widened. "He's mad. What could he do if Eli and I had already wed?"

"Nothing. Except perhaps make you a widow."

Pleasant gasped. "He wouldn't dare!"

Michael's face grew solemn. "Rupert? He would dare. One more reason we came with him—we didn't think it wise to let him go unsupervised. Who knows what sort of mischief he'd cause?"

The sight of Rupert tied to a chair in the hotel dining room, Mrs. Dunnigan and her trusty ladle at the ready should he misbehave, came back, and she chuckled to herself. "I think Rupert has met his match here. He'll be going home empty-handed."

Michael smiled. "Yes, he will." He sighed. "You're happy here?"

She nodded. "More than you know. It's not Comfort Fields by any stretch, but I love the people here. And Eli is a good man. I could do no better."

"I'm glad to hear it. We lost everything, you know—Rupert saw to that. But I have to tell you that Daddy and you were our only concerns."

Pleasant stared at him a moment as her lower lip began to tremble. "You forgive me, then?"

"For what?"

"For running away?"

"Of course we do," Darcy said from behind Michael.

She looked up to find all five of them standing in the kitchen, and smiled in relief. "I didn't mean to hurt anyone when I left, but I just couldn't do it. I couldn't marry Rupert."

"Neither could any of us if we'd been in your shoes," Matt replied. "I'm sorry too. I thought you were being selfish at first. Then I had to think about what I'd do—and I'd have done the same thing."

Pleasant went to her twin and hugged him. "I'm so glad you're here." She pulled away and looked at her brothers. "Stay."

They glanced at one another. "And do what?" Zachary asked. "We have no jobs, no house, nothing."

"And you have the same waiting for you back in Savannah," she pointed out. "Please, now that you're all here, don't leave me."

"Daddy's with Aunt Phidelia," Matt said, more to himself than anyone else.

Benedict went to the worktable, opened the cookie jar, took one out and had a bite. "Mmm, molasses," he said as he chewed. "I'd stay just for these."

Pleasant slapped him on the arm. "Stop that, you! I'm being serious."

"So am I. These are very good." Benedict reached into the jar for another cookie.

"Zachary's right, Pleasant," Darcy said. "We have no means to support ourselves."

"Which is why we have the men's camp," said Grandma as she came out of the patient room.

Pleasant and her brothers stared at her.

"What? It's not that big a house. Can I help it if we can hear just about everything back there?"

"Grandma, how are Eli and my brother?"

"More or less fine. They'll both pull through."

Pleasant sighed in relief. "Can I see them?"

"No, child—let them rest for a spell. You'll see them soon enough."

Benedict set the cookie jar back on the worktable. "That's a relief." He looked at his brothers, then at Grandma. "What is this men's camp?"

"It's where men stay who have no home or steady work yet. They do odd jobs for folks that need help— farming, ranching, building, whatever. After we built the hotel, some of the workers decided they liked it here, and they've been here ever since. They work, pool their money and live together in a big bunkhouse outside of town. One of them's even a full-time cook for the rest. It's not much, I grant, but it'd be a start for you."

"I've never heard of such a thing," Darcy said. He turned to his brothers. "But what about Daddy?"

"I'm sure he's fine with Aunt Phidelia," Pleasant said. "Besides, once you're established, maybe we can send for them and they can come live here too."

Michael scratched the back of his neck. "It's a thought, at least. We'll see what Quince thinks of it."

"Quince?" Grandma said. "Egads, you mean there's more of you?"

"Quince is what they call our eldest brother, Grandma," Pleasant explained. "Everyone else calls him Major, including myself, half the time."

"Oh, I see." She glanced over her shoulder at the door to the patient room. "Well, if my guess is right, I think your older brother will agree to stay."

"What makes you say that?" Pleasant asked.

Grandma winked at her. "Call it a hunch, child. Now let's have tea and cookies."

"Howdy, sweetie," Eli rasped, his eyes half-open. He'd regained consciousness, discovered his midsection had been wrapped like a mail package and asked for his bride. He had no idea how long he'd been out, only that he had to see Pleasant.

She entered, gently sat on the bed next to him and sighed in relief. "How do you feel? Oh wait, that was a stupid question…"

He chuckled. It hurt. "Only natural ya'd ask," he groaned, trying to keep his voice low. He didn't have to work very hard at it—he could barely talk as it was. But he didn't want to risk waking Quince, who was sound asleep on the next bed. "Doc Drake says I'll be good as new in no time."

She took his hand and kissed it. "Don't you ever go out and get yourself shot again!"

He tried to speak, but nothing came out. She had tears in her eyes, and he could tell it was all she could do to hold herself together. He took a breath and slowly let it out. It was enough to get him talking again. "I think… it's what ya call an occupational hazard, sweetie. Sometimes it cain't be helped…" He trailed off.

"Don't talk anymore," she ordered, brushing a lock of hair off his forehead. "We can argue the point later, after you've healed up."

"Yeah, but there's…somethin' that cain't wait."

Her eyebrows knit together. "What?"

"Gettin' married, what else?"

"Married? How can you think about getting married at a time like this?"

Eli smiled weakly. "No time like the present, sweetie. 'Sides, I want ya with me…while I recuperate. Ya cain't stay here…wouldn't be proper."

She laughed. "No, I don't suppose it would." She brushed the same lock of hair away. "Is that what you truly want, Eli?"

"'Course—how ya gonna take care of me otherwise?"

"Take care of you? Oh my…"

"Ya cain't expect Doc and Grandma to keep me here, now can ya? 'Sides, wouldn't ya rather tend me at home? We wouldn't have no privacy with yer brother right there in the next bed."

She stared at him, missing the joke. "Home?"

"Our home…" He really shouldn't talk anymore. Doc had given both he and Quince some laudanum. Quince succumbed to it more quickly, having had whiskey beforehand, but it was starting to bring him down too.

"You're right, I would rather take care of you in our home," she said.

He gave her as much of a smile as he could muster. "Then what are ya waitin' for, sweetie? Go round up Preacher Jo and bring him here…just…soon as… I…" He caught a glimpse of her smile just before he closed his eyes.

She kissed his hand again. Her lips were warm and soft. He could get used to this. "I will," she said, her words pure comfort for him as he drifted off to sleep. She really did live up to her name.

Epilogue

The next day...

"I now pronounce you man and wife," Preacher Jo said happily. "Pleasant, you may *carefully* kiss your husband."

Pleasant sat in a chair next to Eli's bed, his hand in hers as she faced him. She lifted the veil from her face, leaned over, kissed him...and he grimaced. "Oh dear, did I hurt you?"

"Nope," he said. "Gotta cramp in my leg."

Several of Pleasant's brothers laughed, including Quince, who was still in the bed next to Eli's. "Congratulations to you both. I know I speak for us all when I say I hope the two of you will be very happy together."

Pleasant smiled at him then blew him a kiss. "Thank you. That means a lot to me."

"Too bad Daddy couldn't be here to see this," Michael commented.

"Too bad Rupert couldn't," Matt said. "But...he's not feeling very well."

Preacher Jo snorted, then quickly subsided.

Eli eyed him. "What?" He quickly studied the faces of his new brothers-in-law. "What's so funny?"

Benedict was the next to try and stifle his laughter. Harrison and Colin, who had barely managed to squeeze themselves into the room with Sadie and Belle, didn't even try.

"Will somebody tell me what's goin' on?" Eli huffed, then looked at Pleasant in exasperation.

"Well, if you must know," Harrison replied, "dear Mr. Jerney made the mistake of calling your brother Tom a 'dirty pie-eater'."

Eli's mouth dropped open. "That fool did *what*?"

"Worse, he said it in front of Wilfred, Patrick and I," Colin said.

Eli covered his mouth in an attempt not to laugh. If he did, it would hurt. He didn't suffer a broken rib like Quince, but he was sore just the same. "Dirty pie-eater?"

"Where we come from," Quince said, "that's actually quite an insult."

"What does it mean?" Eli asked.

Pleasant glanced at her brothers. "It means…well, it means a stupid country bumpkin. More or less."

"Poor country folk, huh?" Eli said. He looked at Colin. "I suppose you and my brother made sure he knew pie has a whole different meanin' 'round here."

Colin grinned ear to ear. "Oh yes, we certainly did. He won't be eating pie for a while, I'm sure."

Quince glanced at each of his brothers, then at Colin and Harrison. "What exactly does it mean around here?"

Pleasant laughed. "Not what it means back home, that's for certain."

Grandma shoved her way through the crowded room. "We do have kind of a special meaning for it here. Back in '59, our blacksmith Mr. Berg, fell in love, and like all men trying to forget a pretty face, he sought out a distraction."

Quince shrugged. "Which was?"

"The saloon, of course," Grandma said.

"Sounds reasonable," Quince concurred. "But what does that have to do with pie?"

"Mr. Mulligan and Mr. Berg wound up having a pie-eating contest," Harrison explained. "Mrs. Dunnigan had baked a dozen or so for the saloon to last the next few days and they…well, ate them all."

Quince's hand automatically went to his belly. "Ouch! Six pies apiece?"

"Somewhere around that," Colin chortled. "I think Patrick gave up at four and a half."

"Mr. Berg was so sick the next day, he had no problem forgetting his love interest. For a few hours," Grandma concluded.

"So ever since," Colin said with a smile, "pie has symbolized…er…"

"Manly virtue," Harrison offered.

"Quite," Colin agreed. "That is, until your sister recently gave it a new meaning." He arched an eyebrow at Pleasant and Eli.

"It wasn't me!" she said in protest. "It was Eli!"

Most of her brothers laughed, having already heard the story from the Cookes. Quince was left with a puzzled look on his face.

"Where's that scoundrel Rupert now?" Eli asked.

"In his hotel room, sick to his stomach and waiting for the next stage out of town," Harrison said. "Judge Whipple ordered him to leave Clear Creek before he caused any more mischief."

"The judge is here?" Eli asked.

"Sure is," Grandma said. "He's likely to stay a few days, seeing as he's been eating supper with Irene and Wilfred. You know how he loves Irene's cooking. Besides, he's still sentencing those scoundrels. Half of them are wanted for more than just robbery and kidnapping an old lady."

"Thank heaven's the judge listened to Preacher Jo and sentenced Grandma's rescuer to community service at the church," Harrison added.

"Community service?" Eli said.

"Yes, with Preacher Jo and Annie," Grandma confirmed. "Judge Whipple's stomach must not be bothering him or the poor lad might have gotten worse."

More laughter. Eli wanted to laugh too, but didn't dare. Neither did Quince. The two men exchanged a knowing grimace and did their best to sit still.

"You're going to stay on, then?" Colin asked the Comfort men as his chuckles calmed.

The brothers turned to Quince, and he nodded. "For a time, yes. I have to heal, and the rest of us want to help Eli and Pleasant with the addition to their house. We'll do what we can for work and live at the men's camp as Mrs. Waller suggested."

"Call me Grandma, for Heaven's sake! How many times do I have to tell you?"

Quince smiled warmly. "Yes, Grandma."

"That's better," she said. "For a moment I thought I was gonna have to take Irene's ladle to you." The room erupted with laughter once more.

"As far as work, gentlemen, we might need some help with the branding in a couple of weeks," Harrison said. "I'll talk to our foreman about it."

The Comfort men glanced at one another. "None of us has ever done ranch work before, Mr. Cooke," Darcy said. "But we're willing to learn."

"You can learn as you go," Colin said. "There are enough of us to teach you."

"Now that you gentlemen have that settled," Grandma said. "I'm going to go slice the…" She grinned like the devil. "…pies."

Instead of laughing, everyone groaned. Except Grandma, who cackled all the louder and left for the kitchen.

"Belle and I will set the dining table," Sadie said and followed her.

The men were busy chatting about what work the Comfort brothers could find when Honoria stepped into the room. Her eyes darted to Quince before turning to Pleasant and Eli. "Congratulations!"

"Honoria, there you are," Pleasant said. "I wasn't sure if you were going to make it."

"I was in the kitchen getting the wedding lunch ready." She glanced at Quince and swallowed. He watched her with a steady gaze. "I'm afraid I didn't leave a lot of work for Grandma."

"I'm sure she…appreciates it," Pleasant noticed her brother had locked eyes on Honoria. "Um…you are staying of course?"

Honoria swallowed again. "Uh-huh."

Pleasant and Eli looked at Honoria, then at Quince. "Uh-huh," Eli echoed, then leaned as best he could toward his wife. "And it ain't for the pie," he whispered.

Pleasant giggled. "I see that."

As could Harrison. His head snapped back and forth between the two, noting Quince's intense stare and

Honoria's wide doe eyes. "Anyone for pie?" he shouted over everyone's conversations, grabbed his daughter by the hand and ushered her out of the room and into the kitchen.

"Papa!"

"Don't Papa me, young lady!"

She gaped at him. "What did I do?"

He stared at her. Grandma did too, wondering what all the fuss was about. "Harrison? Is everything okay?"

His mouth opened and closed a few times. "Yes," he finally said.

"No," Honoria said. "I want to know why you dragged me out of there. I wasn't done speaking with Pleasant and Eli."

Harrison's eyes skipped between his daughter and Grandma. "I'm sorry, I thought… Grandma needed help."

"What? I already got everything ready," Honoria said in exasperation. She shook her head. "May I go back into the room and finish speaking with Pleasant?"

Harrison sighed as he eyed his daughter. "See what they'd like us to put on their lunch plates."

Honoria nodded, still confused. "I'll be right back."

"See that you do," he said tersely as she left. He started to pace.

Grandma eyed him. "Harrison Cooke, what was that all about?"

"Nothing, absolutely nothing. It was…overcrowded in there, is all."

Grandma folded her arms in front of her. "Uh-huh." She arched an eyebrow and nodded knowingly. "Harrison, you're just going to have to face it."

"Face what?" he said as his pacing ground to a halt.

Grandma noticed he'd clenched his fists. "Honoria is not a little girl anymore."

His jaw tensed as he turned to face her, looking like an angry bull ready to charge. "I'm sure I don't know what you mean," he said, his voice cracking.

"I've seen the way Major Comfort looks at her. And whether you like it or not, Honoria's looking back."

"She's doing nothing of the kind!" He turned away.

"Oh yes she is."

"Not if I have anything to say about it!"

"You might not, son."

He spun to face her, opened his mouth and shook a finger at her, but had no words at the ready.

"What's the matter, Harrison? Cat got your tongue?"

He lowered his hand as his shoulders slumped. "I think perhaps you'd better start baking pies. Lots of them."

Grandma burst into laughter.

"In fact, perhaps I'd better learn how to bake them too."

"Why's that?" she asked through her giggles.

"Because I have a strong feeling that pie is about to take on *another* new meaning around here."

She stopped as she noted his tight jaw and narrowed eyes. "What sort of meaning?"

He met her gaze, his face determined. "Maybe if I eat enough of them, they'll keep me from having to kill, or at least maim, Major Quincy Comfort."

Grandma burst into laughter again. "Harrison, stop! We all knew this day would come."

Harrison growled and marched out of the room just as Sadie and Belle returned from setting the table. "What's the matter with him?" Sadie asked.

"Child," Grandma said, "your husband is about to have his world turned upside down."

Sadie and Belle looked confused. "How so?" Sadie asked cautiously.

"You just wait and see, Sadie. Just wait and see..."

(At least until Harrison learns how to bake pies...)

* * * * *

If you enjoyed Dear Mr. Turner, *then watch for* Dear Mr. Comfort. *Maybe by the time it releases, Harrison will have baked enough pies to make it through the story! And speaking of stories, if you're not familiar with the stories Sadie and Belle talked about with Pleasant, you can find them in the series that started it all,* Prairie Brides, *where you can read about Sadie and Belle's own adventures with their future husbands, Harrison and Colin, not to mention their brother Duncan, the duke. Or as a young Eli Turner used to call him, the duck. Check out the Prairie Bride Series here: http://www.authorkitmorgan.com/prairie-brides/. You'll be glad you did!*

All of Kit Morgan's books can be found at her website, www.authorkitmorgan.com. Be sure to sign up for Kit's newsletter to learn more about upcoming books and special surprises!

About the Author

Kit Morgan, aka Geralyn Beauchamp, lives in a log cabin in the woods in the wonderful state of Oregon. She grew up riding horses, playing cowboys and Indians and has always had a love of Westerns! She and her father watched many Western movies and television shows together, and enjoyed the quirky characters of *Green Acres*. Kit's books have been described as "*Green Acres* meets *Gunsmoke*," and have brought joy and entertainment to thousands of readers. Many of her books are now in audio format, performed by a talented voice actor who brings Kit's characters to life, and can be found on Amazon, Audible.com and iTunes.

Addie kept monopolizing Evan's time. First at the B and B—though
she could hardly blame herself for that. He was the one who'd insisted
on helping her out. And now again at church. Surely he had better
places to be than with her.

"Do you need to go?" she asked Evan. "Sorry I kept you so long."

"I'm not in a rush. I might pop out to Wilder Ranch for lunch with
Jace and Mackenzie. After that I have to…" Evan groaned.

"Run into a burning building? Perform brain surgery? Teach a
sewing class?"

Humor momentarily flashed across his features. "Go to a meeting for
Old Westbend Weekend."

What? So much for some Evan-free time to pull herself back
together. "I'm going to that, but I didn't realize you were. The B and B is
one of the sponsors for the weekend." Addie had used her entire limited
advertising budget for the three-day event.

"I thought my brother might block for me today. Instead he totally
kicked me under the bus as it roared by. He caught Bill's attention and
volunteered me for the hero thing." The pure torment on Evan's face was
almost comical. "I want to back out of it, but Bill played the 'it's for the
kids' card, and now I think I'm trapped."

"Look, Mommy!" Sawyer ran over to them. A grubby, slimy—and very dead—worm rested in the palm of his hand.

"Ew."

At her disgust, Sawyer showed the prize to Evan. "Good find. He looks like he's dead, though, so you'd better give him a proper burial."

"Yeah!" Sawyer hurried over to the patch of dirt. He plopped the worm onto the sidewalk and told it to "stay" just like he would Belay. That made both of them laugh. Then he used one of the sticks as a shovel and began digging a hole.

"He's like a cat, always bringing me dead animals as gifts. I'm surprised he doesn't leave them for me on the doorstep."

Evan chuckled while waving toward the parking lot. She turned to see his brother and Mackenzie walking to their vehicle.

"Do you guys want to come out to Wilder Ranch for lunch? I'm sure they wouldn't mind two more. It's a happy sort of chaos there with all of the kids."

Addie's heart constricted at the offer. No doubt Sawyer would love it. She wanted exactly what Evan was offering, but all of that was off-limits for her. She couldn't allow herself any more access into Evan's world or vice versa.

"We can't, but thanks. I've got to get Sawyer down for a nap." Addie wasn't about to attempt attending a meeting with a tired Sawyer, and she didn't have anywhere else in town for him to go.

Evan's face morphed from relaxed to taut, but he didn't press further. "Right. Okay. I guess I'll see you later then." After saying goodbye to Sawyer, he caught up with Jace and Mackenzie in the parking lot.

A momentary flash of loss ached in Addie's chest. A few days in Evan's presence and he was already showing her how different things could have been. It was like there was a life out there that she'd missed by taking the wrong path. It was shiny and warm and so, so out of reach.

And the worst of it was, until Evan, she hadn't realized just how much she was missing.

Don't miss
Her Hidden Hope *by Jill Lynn,*
available May 2020 wherever
Love Inspired books and ebooks are sold.

LoveInspired.com

LIEXP0420

"Gracie, will you look at me?"

Stifling a sigh, she turned her head to face him. Those melty brown eyes were full of self-recrimination and regret.

"I'm sorry," he said. "I never should have touched you. I'm too old for you, and I'm not any kind of relationship material, anyway. I don't know what got into me, but I swear to you it's never going to happen again."

Hmm. How to respond?

Too bad there wasn't a large blunt object nearby. The guy deserved a hard bop on the head. What was wrong with him? No wonder it hadn't worked out with Marjorie. The man didn't have a clue.

But never mind. Gracie held it together as he apologized some more. She watched that beautiful mouth

HSEEXP0420

move and pondered the mystery of how such a great guy could have his head so far up his own ass.

Maybe if she yanked him close and kissed him, he'd get over himself and admit that last night had been amazing, the two of them had off-the-charts chemistry and he didn't want to walk away from all that goodness, after all.

Yeah, kissing him might shut him up and get him back on track for more hot sexy times. It had worked more than once already.

But come on. She couldn't go jumping on him and smashing her mouth on his every time he started beating himself up for having a good time with her.

No. A girl had to have a little pride.

He thought last night was a mistake?

Fair enough. She'd actually let herself believe for a minute or two there that they had something good going on, that her long dry spell manwise might be over.

But never mind about that. Let him have it his way. She would agree with him.

And then she would show him exactly what he was missing. And then, when he couldn't take it anymore and begged her for another chance, she would say that they couldn't, that he was too old for her and it wouldn't be right.

Don't miss
Their Secret Summer Family *by Christine Rimmer,*
available May 2020 wherever
Harlequin Special Edition books and ebooks are sold.

Harlequin.com

HSEEXP0420

LOVE INSPIRED

INSPIRATIONAL ROMANCE

UPLIFTING STORIES OF FAITH, FORGIVENESS AND HOPE.

Join our social communities to connect with other readers who share your love!

Sign up for the Love Inspired newsletter at **LoveInspired.com** to be the first to find out about upcoming titles, special promotions and exclusive content.

CONNECT WITH US AT:

Facebook.com/LoveInspiredBooks

Twitter.com/LoveInspiredBks

Facebook.com/groups/HarlequinConnection

HARLEQUIN

*Heartfelt or suspenseful,
inspiring or passionate, Harlequin
has your happily-ever-after.*

With new books published
every month, you are sure to find the
satisfying escape you know you deserve.

SIGN UP FOR THE
HARLEQUIN NEWSLETTER

Be the first to hear about great new
reads and exciting offers!

Harlequin.com/newsletters